WICKED PRINCESS

Royal Hearts Academy - Book Three

A. JADE

Wicked Princess
ROYAL HEARTS ACADEMY - BOOK THREE

"The evil queens are the princesses that were never saved."
—Maleficent

Wicked Princess

Cover Design: Lori Jackson at Lori Jackson Design

Editor: Ellie McLove

Rosa Sharon

Kristy Stalter

Prologue

I gesture to the shoebox containing my new ballet slippers. "Are you sure you got the right ones?"

If they aren't the same exact ones Julianna has, it will only give her more ammo to make fun of me.

Mom sighs heavily as she brings her cell phone to her ear and hands the lady at the counter her credit card. "Positive."

She's been on edge more than usual today.

Probably because of the fight she had with my older brother Cole this morning.

Evidently, he wanted to join the peewee football team, but Mom told him no because he's failing all his tests at school.

Annoyed, I look at Cole's twin, Liam.

"Why does Cole always have to ruin everything?"

I expect him to agree because Cole irritates him even more than he irritates me, but Liam simply shrugs.

Thanks to Cole starting with Mom and putting everyone in a bad mood, everything felt *off* today.

I didn't like it.

"Can we get some ice cream?"

Liam wrinkles his nose in disgust.

He claims ice cream is too cold and should be banished from the planet.

I wholeheartedly disagree.

"Come on," I groan, turning my annoyance on him. "I stopped eating meat for you, don't make me give up ice cream too."

Three months ago, he decided he wanted to become a vegan in order to save animals. However, he soon realized he loved cheese too much, so he settled on becoming a vegetarian instead.

Because I love him—and because the video he made me watch of cows being slaughtered gave me nightmares—I agreed to join him.

But ice cream is where I draw the line.

Liam crosses his arms defiantly. "It's too co—"

"No, it's not—"

"Would the two of you stop fighting," our mother snaps as she hastily signs the receipt and throws her phone in her purse. "We are not getting ice cream."

Wow.

"But, Mom—"

"Bianca, please." She gestures to the shopping bags full of leotards. "One more word out of you and so help me God, I'll return everything I just bought."

My mouth drops open in shock.

Not only was it *her* idea to go to the mall today for my new ballet slippers and leotards—she never, ever yelled at me.

Although she loved all her children, it was well known that I was her favorite, and Liam was a close second.

Ever since I could remember, the three of us always had a strong connection.

As if on cue, Liam reaches for my hand.

Cole could be such a big, fat jerk sometimes.

Some days he was so mean she'd end up staying in her bedroom for days at a time.

She claimed she was sick, but we all knew better.

Mom wasn't sick. *She was sad.*

Too bad Jace—our oldest brother—wasn't here.

He always knew the right things to say and what to do.

Given our father was at work all the time, it felt like Jace was more of a dad to me than our actual father was.

However, I only had one mom…and right now she was mad at me.

2

Which made *me* sad.

Her expression softens when she looks at me again. "Bianca."

No. This wasn't fair.

I wasn't like Cole. I never told her I hated her or fought with her. I always told her I loved her...because she's my favorite person.

I *thought* I was hers too.

Unclasping my hand from Liam's, I storm out of the store.

"Bianca, come back here," she yells behind me, but I pick up my pace.

In one fell swoop, she grabs my arm. "I'm sorry."

"You're not my favorite person anymore," I inform her through tears.

"You don't mean that, baby girl."

She was right. I didn't.

Our bond was unbreakable.

But still, the way she treated me before hurt. A lot.

Like Liam, I was sensitive too. Only *unlike* him, I didn't put my weakness on display.

Because my mother told me I needed to be strong.

Stronger than she was.

Spinning me around, she wipes my tears away with her hand. "I love you."

I look down at the floor, unwilling to meet her gaze. "Love you too."

The wall of ice I built thaws as she wraps her arms around me.

She always smelled like warm vanilla and coconut, and her hugs were the best thing in the world.

Like a cocoon.

"You still want that ice cream?"

I nod, clinging to her like a koala.

Out of the corner of my eye, I notice Liam sulking.

I loved my brother more than anything, but he had this annoying habit of wanting everyone to conform to his way of thinking.

Deep down, I knew it was because of his anxiety, but sometimes I ran out of patience.

My mom always understood it though.

Nine times out of ten she was able to stop Liam's meltdowns before they happened.

She untangles one arm from around me and places it around him. "We'll get you some pancakes too, baby. Okay?"

Pancakes were Liam's favorite. But *only* the first two in the stack.

According to him, the rest are never as fluffy and they don't taste as good. *Weirdo.*

Fortunately, Liam agrees. "Fine."

Mom stands up. "Let's haul these bags out to the car and head to the waffle house down the street."

I start to protest, but she adds, "They serve ice cream there too, Bianca."

Yeah, but not the soft serve kind.

Whatever. I'd deal.

We start walking, but she pauses abruptly, glancing at her watch. "Shi—shoot."

"What?"

"I need to stop at the school first."

Liam and I eye one another.

"Why?"

"So she can sign Cole up for football," Liam declares with a sour expression.

"But I thought you told him no?"

She pinches the bridge of her nose. "He really wants this. I've never seen him so—you know what? I'm the mom and what I say goes. I'm signing your brother up for football."

Liam snorts. "You know he'll be bored in a week."

Liam was right. Cole had a tendency to drop out of things quickly.

Mom ruffles his hair. "Well, if he does, maybe *you* can take his place."

Liam looks at her like she sprouted another head as we make our way to the car. "Never. Sports are the worst."

Mom laughs. "They aren't so bad." There's a gleam in her eye when she looks at me. "Who knows, maybe you can be a cheerleader one day just like your mama."

Huh?

"There are cheerleaders in India?" Liam and I ask at the same time.

She laughs again. "Of course there are. Granted, they don't dress like the cheerleaders in America, but—"

The sound of her phone ringing cuts her off.

"Hold that thought," she says, bringing her cell to her ear. "It's your father."

I make mock kissy noises.

My dad might be gone at work a lot, but there's no denying how much he loves her.

He had flowers and chocolates delivered to her almost every day last week.

Liam pouts. "I wish Dad would let us go to India."

"Mom's taking me one day," I tell him smugly as we climb inside the car.

Liam's mouth drops open. "No fair." He looks at Mom. "You have to take me to India too."

Mom shushes him as she peels out of the parking lot.

"She can't," I inform him. "We're going on a mother-daughter trip. Girls only—"

"What the hell is this?" my father's voice booms over the car speakers.

Liam and I exchange another glance. Dad *never* yells at Mom.

"You can read, can't you?" Mom says curtly.

"Rumi," he says, his tone somber. "Talk to me. Tell me what's going on...why you want this."

"I can't right now, Jason. You're on speakerphone and I have your children in the car with me."

"Want *what?*" Liam whispers in my ear.

I was just as confused as him. "I have no idea."

"I'm in Texas for a meeting," Dad states. "But I'll fly home right after, okay?"

"Fine," Mom tells him. "But it won't change anything. My mind is made up."

"Rumi," Dad pleads, like her name is his lifeline. "Please don't do this. I love you—"

"Sorry, Jason. I'm driving through a tunnel. Gotta go."

Eyebrows pinched, Liam looks around. "What tunnel?"

"*W*hat was that about?" Liam hisses.

Mom told us to wait in the car while she ran inside to sign Cole up for football.

I repeat my earlier statement. "I have no idea."

I was only eight. How the heck was *I* supposed to know what our parents were arguing about?

Liam juts his chin. "Mom's on her way back."

I shoot my gaze out the windshield where sure enough, she's walking back to the car, cradling her cell phone against her ear.

But from the looks of her glassy eyes and tense face…it's not a happy conversation.

"She's fighting with Dad again," Liam says, stating the obvious.

"Should we do something?"

"Like what?"

Suddenly Mom stops walking.

"Do you have any idea what I've given up for you?" she screams, snatching the ends of her long dark hair.

My stomach drops.

"India," Liam and I say at the same time.

Mom left her family—and her career as a Bollywood actress—in India to be with him, and she never went back.

The last time she saw her family was their wedding day.

Liam's eyes narrow. "I don't know why Dad won't let her visit them. They're her *family*."

I had an idea as to why, but I wasn't ready to share what I recently overheard just yet.

"Maybe he's protecting her from something?"

"Protecting her from what?"

Here goes nothing. "Last week I overheard Dad—"

A loud sob cuts me off mid-sentence.

Oh, no.

Mom was full-on hysterical crying in the parking lot of our school.

"Crap," Liam says. "Should we go out there?"

I start to nod because Mom's *episodes*—as Jace referred to them—isn't something she'd want on display, but Mom starts walking again.

"Wait. She's coming back."

My relief is short-lived though because she proceeds to kick the side of her car. "I was going to give up *everything* for you!"

"Mom, what are you *doing?*" Liam whisper-shouts, panic rising in his voice as she continues kicking her Mercedes.

Whatever my father was saying to her was sending Mom into an adult temper tantrum.

The worst tantrum I'd ever seen.

"You can't do this to me," she yells, pounding her fists against the hood. "You promised we'd get married and be together forever."

Yeah, our mom was definitely *not* okay right now.

"Maybe we should take Mom's phone away and call Jace?" I suggest.

He'd know what to do.

Liam nods. "Yeah." He eyes me warily. "How?"

I had no freaking idea.

"She's on your side of the car, Liam. Open your door and grab it."

My brother looks at me like I just asked him to kill a python. "Nuh-uh."

Wuss.

"Fine. I'll do it—" I start to say, but the pounding gets worse.

"She's gonna break the window," Liam says, scooching over to my side.

"She's gonna break her *hand.*"

"Don't do this to me," Mom screams so loud we both wince. "I love you, Mark."

Liam and I exchange a wide-eyed glance.

Who the heck is Mark?

"*I*'m fine," Mom says, attempting to wipe away her mascara streaks with the back of her hand.

She tosses her head back and laughs. "Everything is fine."

I clutch Liam's hand. *Everything wasn't fine.*

Mom wasn't acting like herself.

"Can I use your phone?" Liam questions, sticking to the plan to call Jace.

"No," Mom snaps.

So much for that.

I glance out the window in confusion. "Where are we going?"

"The waffle house is the other way," Liam reminds her.

"Don't worry," Mom says. "There will be plenty of pancakes and ice cream soon."

Liam's face lights up. "Are we going to Disney World?"

I pinch his arm.

I had no idea *where* she was taking us, but it wasn't Disney.

"Mom," I begin. "I love you."

Whenever I reminded her how much I loved her, it usually helped calm her down.

"I love you too, baby girl."

"You're going really fast," Liam says. "Slow down."

"It will be all right, baby." A fresh set of tears roll down her cheeks. "Everything will be okay."

Her words offered no relief to either of us.

Liam grips my hand tighter and whispers, "Do you think she's kidnapping us?"

I open my mouth to remind him that Mom wasn't a scary man on the news, she was our mom and therefore couldn't kidnap us... but then I realize he might have a point.

My heart is nearly pounding out of my chest. As much as I complain about my family, I loved them, and I need us all to be together.

"Where are we going?" I croak, my voice trembling.

If I knew where she was taking us, I could call Jace and Cole and tell them what was happening.

"Someplace without pain," she answers as the car begins to swerve.

"Where?" I urge, a bad feeling churning in my stomach.

It feels like forever before she responds.

When she does, it sends a chill down my spine.

"Heaven."

Bile surges up my throat and the hairs on the back of my neck prickle.

For the first time in my life, I finally believed it.

This wasn't normal. *Mom was sick.*

"No," I choke out. "I don't want to go to Heaven."

I wanted to join ballet.

I wanted to get a cat.

I wanted to graduate elementary school.

I wanted to see Dad, Jace, and Cole so I could tell them I love them.

"Mom, please," I plead. "You're just having a bad day."

"A bad *life*." She punches the steering wheel with her fist. "So many things have been taken away from me." Big, ugly sobs fill the car. "I refuse to be without you two."

Turns out being Mom's favorites had its drawbacks.

"You don't have to live without us," Liam tells her. "We'll never leave you."

"It's true," I assure her. "We love you."

More than anything…but I didn't want to die.

"Close your eyes," she instructs as she unclips her seatbelt. "It will all be over soon. I promise."

Liam lets go of my hand and covers his eyes as the car accelerates. "Mommy, stop!"

"Mom, please don't do this!" I cry out, wrapping my arms around my brother. "I love yo—"

Chapter 1

*M*y throat feels like sandpaper, but it's nothing compared to the dull ache coursing through me.

Mom.

Liam.

The thought has my body jerking as I open my eyes.

A white ceiling and harsh florescent lighting greets me.

Where am I?

Where are they?

It's only then I realize someone's holding my hand...sort of.

Mom?

It hurts to turn my head, but I do it anyway.

Confusion impales me as I take in a girl with long brown hair and glasses—who for some unknown reason is painting my nails a bright pink color.

Her warm brown eyes widen, and she jumps up so fast she drops the bottle of polish. "Oh my God. You're...shit. You're *awake.*"

I'm not sure who she is, but she sounds super excited to see me.

She's also *really* short for an adult. Only a few inches taller than I am.

Slowly I take in my surroundings and realize I must be in a hospital.

"Are you a nurse?" I croak, my voice sounding even deeper and raspier than I remember.

She blinks. "I'm Saw—you know what? Let me go get one." Hands shaking, she takes out her cell phone. "I told your brothers to grab some lunch in the cafeteria earlier, but I'm gonna tell them to head back up here pronto." Not stopping for air, she backs out of the room. "You stay right here. I'll be right back, okay?"

It's not like I can go anywhere even if I wanted to.

Between all the IVs, tubes, and machines, not to mention the pain...

Whoa.

My hand looks...different. Not just because of the nail polish the weird nurse used, but it's bigger than I remember and my nails are longer.

I tilt my head down. *Holy cow.*

Mom told me I wouldn't get *those* for at least another four years.

"Hi, honey," a woman wearing scrubs says as she enters the room. "My name is—"

Before she can finish her sentence, some man wearing a lab coat brushes past her. "I'm Dr. Jones."

That's the only introduction I get before he rushes over to my bed and shines a light in my eye. *Geez.*

He points his finger at me. "Follow my finger."

"Where are my mom and brother?"

Placing a stethoscope over my chest, he frowns. "What's your name?"

Shouldn't he already know that?

"Bianca."

"Last name?"

Seriously? "Covington. C-o-v—"

"When is your birthday?"

"June first."

"What year?"

"Two-thousand-two."

"Very good." His eyebrows pinch in concern. "Do you know what today's date is?"

I draw a blank. "No—"

"Bianca!" some man barks as he barrels inside the room.

He's tall with tan skin and short dark hair and his eyes are brown like mine. Only he has dark circles around his, like he hasn't slept in weeks.

He also has a lot of tattoos.

I inwardly shudder. He's kind of scary.

"Holy fuck. You're awake," another man says from behind him before they both surround my bed like a couple of armed guards.

The second guy is also tall with short dark hair. Only unlike the other one, he's pale and his eyes are a very noticeable green...just like my dad's.

For some odd reason, I feel like I *should* know them, but that makes no sense because I've never seen them.

"How are you feeling?" one of them asks.

Like I'm in an alternate universe. "I—"

Before I can answer, the strange, short nurse from earlier trickles in.

"Are my brothers on their way?"

She visibly swallows. "Yeah."

Hopefully they'll be here soon.

My eyes ping-pong between the two guys. They look every bit as baffled as I feel.

"What's wrong with her?" scary guy barks.

Wow. *Rude much?*

I turn my attention to the doctor because I need some answers myself. "Where's my mo—"

"Bianca!" a voice I actually recognize exclaims.

I breathe a sigh of relief as I take the man in. Finally, a familiar face.

"Daddy," I choke out.

Everything is so confusing. I don't know what's going on or where Mom and Liam are.

My dad rushes over and wraps his arms around me. He's hugging me so hard it hurts, but I don't care.

He's the only person in this room I recognize, and I can't help but cling to him like he's my life preserver.

"I'm scared."

Out of the corner of my eye, I see the two men exchange a glance.

For reasons I don't understand, it seems like I've upset them somehow.

"Everything's gonna be okay, sweetheart," my dad assures me. "God, I'm so happy you're all right."

"Where's Mom?" I question. "Is she okay? What about Li—"

"Mom?" one of the guys exclaim. "Bianca, mo—"

"Everyone outside," the doctor instructs.

I try to get off the bed, but sharp shooting pain blazes down my side.

"Not you." The doctor gestures to the woman wearing scrubs. "Nurse Dawn still needs to take your vitals."

As if on cue, the nurse comes over to my bedside.

"Hi, honey. How are you? Is there anything I can get you?"

Remembering my throat feels like a desert, I utter, "Can I have some water?"

"Sure thing." She takes out a thermometer. "I just need to take your temperature first, all right?"

I'm not really in a position to refuse.

After she takes my temperature along with a few other vitals and checks my IV, she hands me a small cup of water.

It feels like heaven...until I hear people arguing right outside my door.

"Is everything okay? Am I in trouble?"

The nurse gives me a reassuring smile. "Of course not, sweetie."

I take another small sip of water. "Why does it hurt to move?"

A crease forms between her brows. "You have a fractured pelvis."

Yikes. "Oh."

She adjusts the pillow beneath me. "The good news is that you're recovering beautifully and as long as that continues, you should be able to start physical therapy in a couple of weeks."

That's great and all, but I have much more pressing issues to worry about.

Clearing my throat, I ask the question no one seems to be answering. "Do you know where my mom and brother are? They were in the car with me when my m—" My mouth clamps shut before I finish that sentence. "Are they okay?"

She pats my hand. "I'm gonna go out there and talk to the

doctor. Are you in any pain right now? Is there anything I can get you? Juice? Maybe some soup?"

I shake my head.

The only thing I want is for her to answer my question, but she ambles out of the room.

A few moments later, the doctor, my father, and the two guys I don't know walk back inside, only there's a new face this time.

A skinny girl with blonde hair and blue eyes.

She's holding the scary guy's hand and rubbing his back... consoling him.

Why?

I look at my father. "What's going on?"

He starts to speak, but Dr. Jones cuts him off.

"Before we get into that, I need to ask you a few questions, okay?"

Again, it's not like I'm in any position to decline.

"Ball, tree, and bird," Dr. Jones states as he looks at his watch. "I want you to remember these words."

Weird. "Okay."

He types something into his tablet. "Bianca, can you tell me where you are?"

I look around. "The hospital...I think."

"Very good." He points to my dad. "And who is this man beside me?"

That's an easy one. "My dad."

He continues typing things on his tablet. "What about the two other gentlemen in the room?"

"I have no idea." I eye them warily. "Should I?"

The scary guy winces and the girl with the blue-streaked hair kisses his shoulder.

A pang of guilt hits me. *They all look so upset.*

"I—I'm sorry."

"You have nothing to be sorry for," Dr. Jones assures me.

Dad's eyes lock with mine. "You didn't do anything wrong, sweetheart."

I didn't but...

Panic rises up my throat.

Mom didn't do anything wrong, either. She wasn't acting like herself.

She loves us. She would never hurt us on purpose.

Another horrifying thought hits me.

Did they take her away? Put her someplace where I'll never be able to see her again?

"I…um."

The room begins to sway, and the cup of water slips out of my hand.

"Where's my mom?"

I need to see her, so I know she's all right.

The scary guy steps forward, only he doesn't look so scary right now.

He looks every bit as terrified as I feel despite the next words out of his mouth.

"Everything will be okay."

The other guy with the piercing green eyes walks over to the other side of my bed. "We got you."

I don't understand any of this. "Who are you?"

The mean one starts to speak again, but Dr. Jones holds up a hand.

"Bianca, can you tell me how old you are?"

"Eight—" I start to answer until I look down again. I certainly don't have the body of an eight-year-old. I don't really *feel* like one either…whatever that means. "I think? I'm not so sure anymore."

Dr. Jones looks up from his tablet. "Can you recall the words I asked you to remember before?"

I scan my brain. "Ball, tree, and bird."

He smiles. "Very good." He looks at my father. "I want to run a few more tests, but it seems her short-term memory is still intact."

"Short term memory?" I repeat, not understanding.

"That's good, right?" scary guy asks.

The doctor nods before he turns his attention back to me. "Can you recall anything about the accident?"

Shaking my head, I clamp my mouth shut.

I don't want Mom to get in trouble.

It wasn't her fault.

Dad frowns. "Nothing at all?"

"Why won't anyone tell me where my mom is?" I look between the two guys standing on opposite sides of my bed. "And who are they? Why are they here? What do they want from me?"

"We're your *brothers*," the guy who looks like my dad barks.

"Cole," the short nurse from earlier hisses. "Calm down before you frighten her."

Too late.

"You aren't my brothers."

Scary guy tries to reach for my hand, but I pull it back.

"Bianca, I know it's confusing and I know you're afraid, but it's true." His brown eyes soften a fraction. "I'm Jace."

"And I'm Cole," the other guy declares.

No. Jace and Cole aren't *this* old.

"That's not possible. Jace is eleven and Cole is ten…so is Liam."

Tears spring to my eyes. *I need to see Liam.* He'd never lie to me.

"I *know* my brothers," I yell, frustration clawing its way up my throat. "You aren't my brothers!" My vision becomes blurry as I peer up at my dad. "Go get my real brothers and my mom."

Dr. Jones claps his hands. "Okay, I think that's enough for now. Everyone needs to give her some space and time to process." He starts ushering them out of the room. "I need to run some more tests. If Bianca's feeling up to it, you can come visit her later."

"I'm not leaving," my dad insists. "She's confused and she needs someone—"

"She needs someone who's not a pseudo-father," someone grunts before the two claiming to be my brothers rush back into the room.

"When you were six, you fell off the jungle gym, cracked your chin open, and needed five stitches," the scary tattoo guy says. "It scared the shit out of Mom. She cried harder than you did."

I rub the faint scar underneath my chin as the memory rushes through my head. "How did you—"

"Because you're my baby sister." He reaches for my hand again. "I was the first person to hold you when you came home from the hospital. The first person to see you take your first steps in the living room, right by the fireplace. I know almost everything about you, Bianca. Like how you slept with a stuffed bear named Mr. Wiggles until you were twelve." Visibly flustered, he points to Cole. "Or how when you were seven, Cole was playing ball in the house and broke Mom's favorite vase, but he told Mom it was you."

That's true. God, I was so mad at him for that.

"Gee, thanks, dick," Cole says before he addresses me. "All right, fine. I blamed you for breaking the vase." He slaps his chest. "But who took the rap when you stole the entire carton of ice cream from Mom's grocery bag and then threw up all over Mrs. Garcia's dog five minutes later?"

"Liam," Jace and I say at the same time.

Cole's jaw works. "Right. But Mom knew Liam hated ice cream, so she didn't believe him. She blamed me."

I can't help but laugh. Cole was pissed when he had to give Mrs. Garcia his weekly allowance so she could get her dog washed and groomed, but I told him he owed me for the vase.

There's no way they'd know any of those things if they weren't Jace and Cole.

I look at Jace who's finally smiling, and I can't believe I didn't realize it until now. "You have Mom's smile."

I turn my attention to Cole next. "And you look like Dad."

He waggles his eyebrows. "Only way better looking, right?"

A laugh flies out of me again because that's totally something Cole would say.

That's when it dawns on me. "Wait a minute…if you guys are all grown up. How old am I?"

They exchange a nervous glance before Jace answers. "Eighteen."

The news feels like ten-thousand bricks to the head.

"I've been in the hospital for ten *years*?"

"Not exactly," Cole mutters before Jace shoots him a warning look.

"What?" I try to sit up in bed, but the pain makes it impossible. "What does that mean?"

Cole sighs. "You've been here for a month."

That only makes me more confused.

"How is that possible? If I'm eighteen like you claim, that means the accident happened ten years ago. But if I've only been here a month—" I stop mid-sentence because there's something way more important that I need them to tell me. "Where is Mom? Where is Liam? Why aren't they here?"

There's no way Mom wouldn't be here.

Jace squeezes my hand. "I know you're confused, but everything will be okay."

"Where is she?"

I'm tired of everyone ignoring my questions about her.

About them.

I turn to Cole. "Where—"

"Cole, *don't*," Jace warns.

Why won't anyone tell me the truth? "Why—"

Oh, God.

The inconsolable expression on Jace and Cole's face twists my insides.

"What happened to her?"

Where are they keeping her?

"Mom—" Jace starts, but his voice catches mid-sentence.

"The accident," Cole says, his voice a broken whisper. "Mom didn't make it."

"No," I scream, refusing to believe it. "You're lying."

She can't be gone.

She wouldn't leave me.

"Bianca—"

It's the last thing I hear before grief sinks its sharp claws into my heart...and everything goes dark.

Chapter 2

*M*y eyelids feel like paperweights, but it's nothing compared to the boulder of anguish on my chest.

She's gone.

I'm never going to see her again.

"I told you she needed time to process everything," some man says sternly.

It sounds like he's standing right outside my door.

"She deserved to know the truth," someone who sounds a lot like Cole argues.

"It was too early," Jace whispers. "She couldn't handle it."

"Precisely," the man says. "I don't even know the extent of her brain injury yet and you two just…" He sighs long and deep. "Think of your sister like a broken puzzle. She has certain pieces, but not enough to make up the entirety of it. Right now, her reality is just that. *Her* reality. The only accident she remembers is the one with your mother. Her brain is stuck in that trauma and it's important for her family to understand this because if she does get her memory back—"

"What do you mean *if*?" Jace barks.

"Are you telling me this amnesia is permanent?" someone who sounds like my dad asks.

There's another long sigh. "There's no way to tell right now. But you have to be careful not to feed her information—"

"Why?" Cole questions. "If she can't remember, why is telling her such a bad thing?"

"Because you're giving her *your* biased memories and thoughts. You're not giving her a chance to heal and remember hers. The brain is a very complex, very *sensitive* organ. Influencing her memory and pushing her too hard, too fast will only make things worse."

"So what should we do?" Jace asks. "How do we help her get better?"

"Time and patience. Lots of it. Her memories—if she gets them back—might be distorted, but it's important not to argue or correct her." He clears his throat. "In the meantime, I've taken the liberty of contacting Dr. Wilson. He's a top-notch psychologist who has a lot of experience working with patients who have brain injuries and amnesia. Given the severity of Bianca's mental state and what's happened, I think it's important she talks to someone. Fortunately, he's agreed to come up to the hospital to meet with her this week."

My eyes flutter open as Dr. Jones ambles inside the room and walks over to my bed. "Hello, Bianca. How are you feeling?"

Like I've been run over by a bus.

"Tired."

He nods. "That's the sedative."

"Sedative? Why—"

I stop talking as images of me ripping out my IV and then punching Jace and Cole flash through my head.

A stabbing pain infiltrates my heart. "My mom...she's—"

I can't say the words.

Saying the words out loud will only give them credence.

Instead, I lunge for the doctor.

Not because I want to hurt him.

I just want him to give me something to make me go numb.

Something to help me forget the truth burrowing through my veins.

Not only is my mom dead...

She killed Liam.

Chapter 3

Past...

"*I* m-m-miss her," Liam whispers. Ever since the accident, he developed a horrible stutter.

According to Dr. Young—our mother's therapist—it's due to the trauma of not only the accident but losing Mom.

Tilting my head, I turn to look at my brother. "Me too."

It's been almost a month since Mom passed away and every day feels harder than the last.

Liam sighs. "D-d-do you think s-s-she's happy in Heaven?"

"I hope so."

A tear rolls down his cheek. "W-w-why'd s-s-she leave us? W-w-why w-w-weren't we g-g-good enough?"

"I don't know," I answer honestly, wiping his tears away with my sleeve.

He sniffles. "I w-w-want to t-t-tell Dad."

Panic zips up my spine. "You can't."

His face scrunches. "W-w-why?"

"Stop being dumb. You *know* why."

Mom loved us. She doesn't deserve to be remembered by her mistakes.

However, if people found out the truth, that's all they'd remember her for.

They'll blame her and say mean things about her.

Plus, my family is already so sad over losing Mom and knowing what really happened that day will only make everyone's pain worse.

Liam and I made a pact to protect her and he wasn't allowed to break it.

"Sometimes you have to lie to protect the people you love, Liam."

It was something I heard on TV one day, but it never really made sense to me until the accident.

Until after she was gone.

"I know. It j-j-just gets s-s-so hard s-s-sometimes." His lower lip trembles. "And p-p-people at s-s-school…they…" He shakes his head. "Never m-m-mind."

Liam was known for being sensitive, but there was something more happening here.

"What's going on?"

He turns away, like he's trying to avoid my gaze, but I don't let him. "You can tell me anything, Liam. You know that."

Now that Mom was gone, he was officially my bestest friend in the whole wide world.

I'd always keep his secrets.

He points to his face. "They k-k-keep c-c-calling me a m-m-monster."

My heart folds in on itself. Not only did Liam develop a stutter from the accident, he also has a few facial scars from the glass.

It made the kidney I lost seem like a walk in the park because at least I could hide my injury.

Liam wasn't so lucky.

I trace the large pink scar over his cheekbone, wishing I could make it disappear. "You're not a monster."

He was the farthest thing from one. He was kind and compassionate…and sad.

Just like Mom.

"Y-y-yes I am." He scowls. "No one l-l-likes m-m-me."

I'm about to remind him that his family likes him, but then he whispers, "E-e-except her."

"Who?"

He grins. "Dylan."

Oh, boy. I walked right into that one.

About a week ago Jace brought home some girl he met at school. The two have been inseparable ever since.

Cole teased him about liking his new friend, but Jace claims she's just really good at video games.

Given he beats Dylan every time they play though, I'm starting to have my doubts.

Then again, if he liked her, he'd probably let her win. *I think.*

I'm not really sure how it works. I think all boys are gross and have cooties.

"S-s-she's s-s-so pretty," Liam says. "And s-s-so s-s-smart and c-c-cool. And s-s-she doesn't m-m-make fun of m-m-me." His grin grows. "S-s-she's perfect."

I want to remind him how Mom always told us that *no one* is perfect, but it's no use. He's so far gone there's no talking any sense into him.

I roll my eyes. "You've got it bad, dude."

Worse than bad. He's practically *obsessed* with her.

He doesn't argue. "I'm g-g-gonna m-m-marry her one day. You'll s-s-see."

Oh boy. If I don't stop him now, he'll go on and on about her until sunrise.

"Here's an idea. How about you don't force me to listen to you talk about Dylan for the rest of the night."

"Whatever." He studies my face. "W-w-why don't w-w-we t-t-talk about how you're s-s-still too s-s-scared to g-g-go in the c-c-car?"

Nope. Not happening.

I cup my hand over my ear as I get off the bed. "What's that, Jace? You need help doing laundry?"

I'd rather do a lifetime of chores than talk about my newfound fear of cars.

Liam frowns. "Bianca—"

I don't hear the rest of his statement because I run out the door.

Chapter 4

"*L*iam didn't die," I yell as my eyes flutter open. "He couldn't have. I talked to him after the accident."

He's still alive.

It's a small ray of hope in a mountain of grief, but it feels so good.

Like a rainbow after a storm.

Standing at the foot of my bed, Jace and Cole exchange a glance.

"What do you mean you talked to him?" Cole questions.

"In my dream...I think." I shake my head. "I don't know but it felt real."

Too real.

Jace plops down in the chair beside me. "What did you two talk about?"

Given I can't tell them what happened to Mom because of our pact, I tell them the next best thing.

"Dylan. He has a crush on her."

Jace winces. "Oh."

Cole sucks in a sharp breath. "Yeah, that wasn't a dream."

"I know," I exclaim, excitement rushing through me. "He's alive." For the first time in three days, I smile. "Where is he?"

It's weird he hasn't come up to see me. Then again, maybe he did, and I didn't notice because of all the sedatives.

Jace and Cole exchange another glance before Jace speaks.

"Liam didn't die during the accident, but—"

"He's away at school," Cole interjects. "He's been busy with his exams and shit, but he'll be up to see you soon."

I'm so happy I could cry. "Really?"

Jace shoots Cole a murderous glare. "Outside. *Now*."

I have no idea what that's about, but it doesn't matter.

Liam's alive.

"Hey," Sawyer—who's apparently not a nurse, but Cole's fiancée —greets me from the door. "Can I come in?"

Truth be told, I can't believe he managed to snag someone as awesome as Sawyer, but I'm happy for him.

Given I can use the company, I wave her in. "Of course."

Evidently, she's not alone though because the girl who's always hanging around Jace is right behind her.

I'm not sure what to make of Jace's friend because she's super quiet and standoffish.

Then again, I've been flipping out and attacking everyone for the last five days, so I can't really blame her.

"How are you feeling?" Sawyer asks, taking a tentative step in my direction.

"Better." Annoyance colors my tone. "But I'm getting *really* sick of Jell-O, pudding, apples, and vegetable soup."

I'm beginning to think it's the only shit they serve in this freaking hospital.

She hikes a thumb behind her. "I can go get you something—"

"No," I say in a rush. "Please don't leave. I love my brothers and all, but they can be a little—"

"Protective?" Sawyer supplies.

"Overbearing?" the other girl chimes in.

I can't help but laugh because it's obvious they both know them well. "Exactly." Embarrassed, I decide to bring up the elephant in the room. "I'm sorry I've been acting crazy. I just—"

"No need to apologize. It's totally understandable," Sawyer says as she takes a seat on the chair beside my bed.

I can't help but notice how pretty she is. Maybe not in the conventional sense like a model, but in the way that really counts.

On the inside.

She looks like she wants to give me a hug but thinks better of it. "You've been through a lot."

There's a kindness that emanates from her and I can't help but feel at ease in her presence.

I'm not sure why or where it's coming from, but something tells me she's a good person and I can trust her.

"No wonder my brother's in love with you." I rise up on my elbows, attempting to stretch a little because being bedridden sucks. "Not only are you gorgeous, but you seem really easy to talk to."

Knowing I have to make an effort with Jace's girl too, I turn my focus on her.

Unlike Sawyer, who's wearing a cardigan and long skirt, this girl is wearing tight jeans, boots, and what looks like an old black t-shirt with some faded decal on it.

Her outfit would look weird on anyone else, but somehow, she makes it work.

"You have great style." I give her a genuine smile so she doesn't think I'm bullshitting. "Maybe when they let me out of here, we can go shopping sometime."

The girl and Sawyer exchange a wide-eyed glance that seems to last forever.

That's...*unnerving*. "Did I say something wrong?"

I was just trying to make a good impression and get to know them a little.

"No," Sawyer assures me. "You didn't say *anything* wrong."

Sawyer gives her a look, prompting her to speak.

The girl crosses her arms. "I'm gonna go check on Jace."

It doesn't take a genius to figure out this girl isn't my biggest fan.

I don't understand why though because we hardly even know each other.

Maybe it's time to change that.

I decide to start with the basics. "I'm sorry, I never caught your name before."

The girl stops to look at me. "Dylan."

I study her features for what feels like an eternity and that's when it dawns on me.

Well, shit.

She's *the* Dylan.

"*You're* Jace's girlfriend?" I clarify as she bolts for the door.

She stops short. "Yup."

"They live together," Sawyer adds.

If that's the case, she must make Jace happy. I just hope it wasn't at the expense of *Liam's* happiness.

A peculiar thought hits me.

Maybe it's why he hasn't shown up.

Maybe it hurts too much to see them together.

"How does my brother feel about this?"

Dylan raises an eyebrow. "I'm pretty sure Jace—"

"Not Jace," I clarify. "How does *Liam* feel about you and Jace being together?"

She has to know he's in love with her. It's obvious to anyone with a pulse.

The girl turns ashen, like she's just seen a ghost, and then quick as lightning…she's gone.

My eyes flick to Sawyer. "I don't—"

"Hey," Jace says, entering the room. He gestures to the tray he's holding. "Lunch is here."

"What is it?"

I *really* hope it's not vegetable soup or another apple.

He inspects the tray. "Well, there's chocolate pudding." He places the tray on the table beside me. "And your favorite—vegetable soup and an apple."

Ugh. Pretty soon I'm going to turn into apples and vegetable soup.

"Thanks." Reaching over, I pick up the spoon, opting for the chocolate pudding instead. "I'm not trying to be mean or anything, but I don't think it's a good idea for her to come here anymore."

She ran away like a bat out of hell when I brought up Liam which can only mean one thing.

She hurt Liam.

Jace's eyebrows pinch. "Who?"

"Dylan."

His jaw tics. "Why?"

"Because she's the reason Liam hasn't shown up. He doesn't want to see you two together, Jace, and I can't blame him. It can't be easy watching your own brother be with the girl you love."

His face falls. There's so much agony in his eyes it makes me want to take the words back.

But I won't. Because someone has to stick up for Liam.

Be his voice when he doesn't have one.

"Yeah," he says softly. "Yeah, okay. If that's what you want, I'll tell her not to come up here anymore."

"Jace." Sawyer glares at him. "I really don't think that's—"

He holds up a hand, cutting her off. "I'm gonna go check…" His sentence trails off as he backs out of the room.

Chapter 5

"*I* wasn't trying to upset him. I love Jace and I want him to be happy. I just don't want Liam to feel like he can't be around his family, you know?"

Dr. Wilson—or Walter as he told me to call him—jots something down in his notebook. "Let me get this straight. You think if Dylan keeps her distance, Liam will come visit you."

"I hope so." A pang of sadness shoots through my heart. "Jace and Liam weren't just brothers, they were *friends*. It can't be easy for Liam to see him with Dylan."

"Just to make sure I understand—in your mind, keeping Dylan away from Jace protects Liam."

Eureka. Finally, he's starting to get it.

"And Jace," I clarify. "Given she hurt Liam, who's to say she won't hurt Jace one day, too?"

He folds his hands. "I see." He clears his throat. "Now that we've got that squared away for now, I think it's important we talk about your mother."

And just like that, pain wraps around my heart, squeezing me so tight I can barely breathe.

"You said I didn't have to talk about anything I didn't want to," I remind him.

"That's correct."

"Well, I don't want to talk about her. Not today."

Not ever.

It hurts too much.

"Have you figured out why she's not eating yet, doc?" Cole interjects from the doorway of my room.

Dr. Wilson looks at me. "You aren't eating?"

As if on cue, Jace pops up behind Cole. "Not since yesterday morning."

Tattletales.

The psychiatrist adjusts his glasses. "Why aren't you eating, Bianca?"

"I'm just not hungry, Walter."

Truth is, I'm starving, I'm just so sick of what they're serving here.

And sure, Jace and Cole have brought me outside food, but it isn't any better.

Just a bunch of fruit, veggies, and other gross, bland, healthy stuff.

If I didn't know any better, I'd think they were subliminally trying to get me to lose weight, but according to my nurse I've never been overweight, and I've lost seven pounds since I've been here.

Therefore, I'm really not sure why they're shoving all this healthy crap down my throat every day, but I wish it would stop.

Walter strokes his chin as if pondering something. "If you could have anything in the world to eat right now, what would it be?"

It takes me less than two seconds to answer. "A big, greasy, bacon cheeseburger with ketchup and mayonnaise." I drum my nails on the railing of my bed. "And a big side of fries and pickles."

My stomach roars to life, growling its approval.

"I see," Walter says, jotting something else in his notebook.

Jace and Cole's mouths drop open.

"You want a burger?" Cole exclaims. "Like a *real* one?"

Well, I certainly don't want a fake one.

"Are you *sure*?" Jace questions.

"Positive." A pang of guilt hits me. "I know you guys want me to eat super healthy and stuff but—"

Cole starts laughing. "No, we don't."

Color me confused. "You don't?"

34

Jace shakes his head. "Bianca, you're a vegetarian and a devout health food nut." Jace's lips twitch. "I can't even recall the last time you ate a potato chip."

This is news to me. "Really?"

"Yeah…or at least you were." He looks at Walter. "Is this normal?"

He nods. "It's not uncommon for those with head injuries to have personality and other changes."

Jace and Cole exchange a glance.

"Makes sense," Cole mutters.

Jace nods in agreement. "Definitely."

I hate feeling like I'm the butt of an inside joke that I have absolutely no recollection of. "Care to share with the class?"

Shrugging, Jace shoves his hands in the pocket of his hoodie. "It's nothing bad. You've just been a little…you know…different."

"The word you're looking for is nice," Cole mutters.

Hold the phone.

I've attacked my poor doctor and nurse, not to mention *them* last week and they think *that* was nice?

Cole starts to speak again, but Jace clamps a hand on his shoulder. "Let's put this conversation on the backburner for a minute so we can go grab her that burger."

Cole grins. "We should go get her one from Fatty's."

I have no idea what Fatty's is, but I'll eat just about anything as long as it's not healthy.

"It's the best burger you'll ever have," Cole declares as they head for the door. "Are you sure you want pickles though? You used to have a phobia of them."

"A phobia of pickles?"

Jace laughs. "Yeah. When you were five, you got it in your head that pickles were really dead frogs in a jar, and you were terrified to eat them."

I have no recollection of that at all. "That's so…*weird.*"

Not to mention, it makes no sense.

"Tell me about it," Cole says. "But it was funny as fuck watching you scream at people to stop eating the frogs whenever Mom and Dad took us to a restaurant."

I bet.

Walter stands up. "I have another appointment, but what do you say I stop by in a few days so we can talk some more?"

"Sure." I gesture to my bed. "I'll be here."

Wondering who the girl I used to be was and what happened to her.

Chapter 6

"*I*s there anything I can get you?" Sawyer asks. "Anything I can do?"

Aside from bringing my mom back from the dead and locating Liam...nope.

I stare up at the ceiling. "No."

"How about you let me do your makeup?" she suggests. "Or paint your nails again?"

With the way she keeps bringing up makeup and nails, I'm starting to think I must have been *very* into that stuff.

"No thanks." Turning my head, I look at her. "Sawyer?"

"Yeah?"

"Where's Liam?"

It's been a week since I found out he's alive but there's still no sign of my brother.

The world feels cold and lonely without him.

Like someone shut off the sun.

She frowns. "I—"

Whatever she was going to say fades away when Cole walks into the room.

"Hey." He gestures to the paper bag with grease stains he's holding. "I brought you a burger and fries." He grins. "No pickles."

"No thanks."

I close my eyes, silently wishing everyone would leave me alone.

37

"What's wrong?"

"She misses Liam," Sawyer tells him.

More than miss.

I feel like I lost a vital part of myself.

"I'm really tired," I grind out, hoping they take the hint.

"We'll let you get some sleep." Sawyer squeezes my hand. "If you need anything, let us know."

I need Liam.

Past...

"*D*o you t-t-think Mom w-w-went t-t-to Heaven?" Liam whispers into the darkness.

I glare at my brother's shadowy face. "Of course she went to Heaven. Why would you think otherwise?"

It's been almost six months since our mom died and the pain isn't any better.

Sometimes it hurts so bad I force Liam to sleep in my bedroom.

Chase the nightmares away.

"Drew Harrison," Liam tells me matter-of-factly. "He s-s-said if s-s-someone c-c-commits s-s-suicide they go to Hell."

"Drew Harrison is an idiot." I drop my voice to a whisper so only he can hear me. "Besides, Mom didn't commit suicide."

Liam's brows furrow. "Yes, s-s-she—"

"No, she *didn't*," I argue, flicking on the small lamp on my nightstand. "She didn't want to die that day. She just wanted the pain to end. Big difference."

There had to be.

Turning on my mattress, he stares up at my bedroom ceiling. "Yeah, I guess you're r-r-right." He blows out a heavy breath. "Bianca?"

"Yeah?"

"Who do you think Mark is?"

My heart clenches. "I have no idea."

And I'm not so sure I want to.

"She s-s-said she loved him," Liam whispers.

"So."

Mom was a good person. She loved lots of people.

He gives me a pointed look. "W-w-what about Dad?"

"What about Dad?"

I have no idea what he's hinting at.

His forehead creases. "W-w-what if Dad w-w-wasn't the only m-m-man M-m-mom loved?"

Rage grows so thick in my throat it practically chokes me.

Before I can stop myself, I launch my fist into his arm. "Daddy is her husband, dummy."

"Ouch," Liam cries out. "T-t-that hurts."

I punch him again. Harder this time. "Take it back."

"No." Scowling, he gets off the bed. "I w-w-want to t-t-tell Dad the t-t-truth."

A knot of dread coils in my stomach. "You promised."

Tears cloud his eyes. "And M-m-mom always promised t-t-that s-s-she loved us." He rams his fist into his chest. "But s-s-she left us. She t-t-tried to k-k-ki—"

I cover his mouth with my hand before he finishes that statement.

"She was sick, Liam. The kind of sick people can't see because it was in her brain."

I've been researching all sorts of things since the accident.

Trying to figure out what was wrong with her.

Why she felt leaving was the only option.

I don't understand a lot of it right now, but there was something wrong with my mom's mind.

It didn't work like it should, and it made her sad a lot.

So sad nothing could make her happy.

Not even her own children.

"Maybe I'm s-s-sick t-t-too." He looks down at the floor. "S-s-sometimes I t-t-think about leaving like s-s-she did."

A ball of hurt seizes my heart, sending everything spiraling.

He can't.

Liam is the only one who understands.

I start shaking as tears run down my cheeks. "You can't be serious."

Sadness flickers in Liam's eyes, but he doesn't say a word.

No. He can't do this.

He's my favorite person.

"You can't leave me," I choke out, my voice coming out like broken glass. "You can't. You're my fav—"

In one fell swoop, he wraps his arms around me, hugging me tight.

"I know. I w-w-was being s-s-stupid. I'm s-s-sorry."

Not good enough.

"Promise me," I hiss, holding up my pinky finger. "Promise me you'll stay with me. No matter how bad it gets or how much it hurts."

I need him to swear we're in this together. *Always.*

Relief fills me as he links his pinky with mine. "Promise."

Chapter 7

*T*he room is dark when I open my eyes and the uneaten tray of food on my tray table tells me I must have slept straight through dinner.

I reach for the new phone Jace got me since mine was destroyed in the accident, but I notice a tall, shadowy figure in my peripheral vision.

"Jesus."

"H-h-hey."

I nearly swallow my tongue when I realize. "Holy shit. *Liam?*"

Despite the pain coursing through my hips and thighs, I sit up in bed.

"You're here."

No surprise, the adult version of Liam looks just like his identical twin.

God, there are so many things I want to say, but I have no idea where to begin. It feels like an eternity since I've seen him.

"How are y-y-you feeling?" he asks after another moment passes.

"Okay, I guess...considering." I give him the biggest smile I can muster. "Better now that you're here."

"That's—" He clears his throat. "T-t-that's good."

I decide to make small talk to break the ice. "How's school?"

He shrugs. "Fine."

He's a lot less talkative than I remember.

Then again, I'd have no idea what to say to someone who lost their memory either.

"I have something called retrograde amnesia," I tell him, because I'm not sure what else to talk about.

Concern lines his features. "I k-k-know."

An awkward silence stretches between us for what feels like forever and I can't help but wonder why my favorite person suddenly feels like a stranger.

"Are you mad at me?"

I need to know why things feel so strange between us.

Why he won't look me in the eye.

Why he looks so miserable right now.

Like he hates himself for being here.

Rocking back on his heels, he shoves his hands in the pockets of his sweatpants. "No."

My heart sinks because the Liam I remember was a mush who would have wrapped me up in a big bear hug and assured me everything was fine.

This Liam is detached and distant.

Almost cold.

Like he can't stand to be near me.

Peering up at him, I study his face.

He has the same sharp features, same ink-black hair, same green eyes, same pale skin with scars…wait a minute.

"Your scars. They're gone."

His eyes widen. "I-uh…I used a r-r-really good c-c-cream."

The sinking feeling in the pit of my stomach intensifies.

I might not remember most things, but I trust my instincts enough to know this feels all wrong.

"Liam?"

"Yeah?"

"Why are you acting so different?"

He crosses his arms. "I'm not acting different."

Liam looks as surprised as I feel when a sob breaks through the tension.

Everything in my life is upside down, so I don't know why I expected any less when it came to him.

Maybe it's because I always thought of him as my constant, and therefore never figured our bond could be broken.

But it is.

"I'm sorry," I choke out, wiping my tears with the back of my hand. "I'm just really emo—"

The hug comes then, but that feels different too.

"Please don't cry," he whispers. "I didn't mean to hurt you."

He sounds so earnest, I'm the one feeling bad now.

"It's not your fault. My emotions are all over the place lately." I grab a tissue from the box. "I feel like someone stuck my life in a snow globe and shook it."

Only instead of creating something enchanting and beautiful... it's just one big, ugly mess.

"I know everything sucks balls right now." He kisses the top of my head. "But you are going to be fine."

I wish I had the bright outlook he does. "I'm not so sure about that."

"Come on." He grins. "You're a Covington, dammit. We're resilient assholes who survived the worst things imaginable then stood up and asked the universe if that was all they had because they hit like a little bitch."

I start to laugh...until it hits me.

Not only is he not stuttering anymore, that sounds exactly like something *Cole* would say.

I stare down at the logo on his t-shirt.

Liam doesn't like sports, therefore he wouldn't be caught dead wearing a *Patriots* t-shirt.

"You're not Liam."

Cole has the good grace to look sheepish. "You're right." He blows out a breath. "I'm not."

I close my eyes against the surge of anger streaming through me. "Why the hell would you pretend to be—"

The door opens and the light flicks on.

"Everything okay?" Jace questions, his gaze ping-ponging between us.

Cole tries to speak, but I don't give him the chance.

"No, it's not." I glare at Cole. "Cole tricked me into thinking he was Liam."

Jace looks like it's taking every ounce of his strength not to walk over and throttle him. "You did *what?*" Eyes narrowed, he takes a step closer. "Why the fuck would you do that?"

Muttering a curse, Cole pinches the bridge of his nose. "I was only trying to help—"

"Help? How the *fuck* is pretending to be Liam going to help her recover?" Jace roars. "I told you we needed to listen to the doctors."

Well, shit. Jace seems mad enough for the both of us.

However, I don't need him to fight this battle for me because while I don't understand why he pretended to be his twin; it's obvious Cole meant no harm.

I'm about to tell them both to calm down, but Cole grunts, "I know we're supposed to listen to the doctors, but she was really upset earlier. I thought...I don't know. I was just trying to give her a little normal before—"

"Before what?" I question, because it's clear I've been left in the dark about something.

Or rather, *someone.*

"Where's Liam?"

"Good job, asshole," Jace mutters before he looks at me. "Everything is fine."

"Don't lie to me." I look at Cole. "Why were you pretending to be Liam?"

Jace shoots him a murderous glare. "Hallway. *Now.*"

"No," I snap. "So help me God one of you better tell me wh—"

Pain pulses through my temples. It's so severe, it renders me breathless.

Something's wrong.

Jace is saying something, but I don't hear him.

I'm too scared.

I pound on the tray table. "Let me in!"

Past...

"*W*hat's going on?" I scream, the fear nearly crippling me.

"Go downstairs and call 911!" Jace yells on the other side of Liam's bedroom door.

I'm so scared I can barely breathe.

What happened to him?

Heart and stomach full of terror, I run down the staircase on unsteady legs and make a beeline for the phone in the kitchen.

My fingers shake so bad, I drop the phone before punching in the numbers.

"911, what's your emergency?" some lady on the other line answers.

"I need—" My voice is so jittery I can barely speak.

I clear my throat and try again. "I need an ambulance for my brother." Remembering the time Mom spent two whole days teaching me our address in case of an emergency, I quickly add, "We live at 101 Royal Manor Lane. Please come quick."

"Got it. Can you tell me what happened, sweetie?"

Didn't she hear me before?

"Something is wrong with my brother. He's twelve."

"Okay, honey. An ambulance is on the way. Do you know what happened so I can tell the EMTs?"

"I don't know," I scream. "No one will tell me. Please hurry."

I quickly drop the phone and head back upstairs.

I need to see Liam.

I can make him better.

"The ambulance is on the way." I pound on the door. "Let me in."

I need to make sure he's okay.

"Go downstairs," Jace shouts.

"No."

There's no way I'd ever leave him, especially if he's in pain.

It's when he needs me the most.

"I want to see Liam."

"Bianca, go downstairs," Jace screams again, but his voice doesn't sound right.

He's crying.

My stomach falls and sheer panic zips up my spine.

Jace never cries.

"Liam!!" I yell, banging on the door harder. "Liam, come out here!"

I have to see him.

My heart squeezes like a vise and tears clog my vision. "I want to see Liam."

Why won't they let me see him?

I start kicking the door. "Liam!"

I'm here, Liam.

I'm right here.

Everything's gonna be okay.

We're in this together.

The doorknob turns and I don't waste another second. I push it open with every ounce of strength I have.

Strength that leaves me in one big gust a second later.

This can't be happening.

This isn't real.

Five minutes ago, Jace was making him his favorite—pancakes.

And now...

I scream so loud my ears ring as I take in his stiff, blue-tinged body lying on the floor of his closet.

"Liam!" His name rips out of my vocal cords, burning my insides.

Answer me.

Wake up and answer me.

But he can't.

"Dammit," Jace hisses.

A deep, wide wave of pain spreads throughout my chest, gripping me by the throat until I'm trembling.

He pinky swore.

In one fell swoop, Cole picks me up and heads for the staircase.

I kick and scream the whole way down, not wanting to be away from my favorite person.

Even though he's no longer here.

"I'm sorry," Cole whispers.

All I can do is cry. As if my tears and agony alone could bring him back.

But they won't.

Because Liam broke his promise.

Broke what was left of me.

Chapter 8

*G*iving me a hopeful smile, Jace squeezes my arm. "We brought you breakfast."

As if on cue, Cole holds up a paper bag. "Sausage and eggs."

I close my eyes, willing them to go away.

"It's been over a week, Jace," Cole mutters. "She's not snapping out of this."

Jace sighs. "I know."

I draw in a sharp agonizing breath as their footsteps fade, wishing it would wash all the pain away.

He left me without warning.

One second we were waiting for him to join us for breakfast and making plans to go to the mall…and the next he was gone.

Just like our mother.

"Fuck this," Jace grunts before I hear the footsteps returning to my room. "I'm not losing her too."

"Go away," I choke out.

I don't want to talk.

I don't want to breathe.

I don't want to live in a world in which he no longer exists.

If God had any compassion, he would have taken me too.

Jace crosses his arms. "No."

Cole matches his stance. "Make us."

Their stubbornness would almost be comical if my heart didn't feel like someone took a blowtorch to it.

"He left me," I whisper, a fresh wave of agony swelling in my chest.

He knew I couldn't survive without him.

He knew I wouldn't make it on my own.

"He left all of us," Cole bites out, towering over me.

Cole's always been a moody jerk, but right now he's pissing me off more than usual.

I glare at him. "Go *away*."

"Cole's right," Jace interjects and the pain reflecting in his eyes mirrors my own. "But as much as it hurts, you *have* to find a way to go on."

How?

How the hell do you go on living when the two most important people in your life are dead?

How do you wake up to face a brand-new day without the constant reminder of everything you lost?

How do you move past all the pain?

Easy. *You don't.*

Because time doesn't heal all wounds.

It just leaves you with scars.

"I can't." I don't bother wiping the tear that slides down my cheek. "I don't have a reason to."

Not anymore.

I have no mom, no Liam…and the only memories I have cause me a heart full of what feels like non-stop suffering.

A loud crash makes me jump.

"Fuck you," Jace bites out, seething with anger.

"I—"

He punches his chest with his fist. "You have us, Bianca. You still have *us*."

Something uncomfortable churns in my belly.

Guilt, I realize.

Because the heartbroken look on his face tells me how much what I said hurt him.

I notice Cole's wounded expression and inwardly flinch. *Hurt them both.*

"I know how much you miss them." Cole shrugs helplessly. "But Jace and I…we're still here. That has to count for something, right?"

Regret and shame tangle in my chest. I never meant to make them feel like they didn't matter.

"I'm sorry."

Even though losing Mom and Liam hurts like hell, I have two very important reasons to try and put one step in front of the other and pull myself together.

"Don't be sorry," Jace says. "Just be here with us." His gaze ping-pongs between Cole and me. "Because even though they're gone, we're *still* a family."

Nodding, Cole turns his focus on me. "Look, I'm not gonna stand here and promise to be a perfect brother like Liam was and Jace is. But I'll do whatever it takes to help you through this. Deal?"

I tilt my chin to meet his gaze. "Deal."

"Good." He gestures to the bag containing my breakfast. "Now eat that before it gets cold."

I look at Jace. "Is he always so bossy?"

His lips twitch. "Yup." He takes the breakfast sandwich out of the bag and places it on my meal tray. "He gets it from me. Now *eat.*"

I'm torn between wanting to laugh and wanting to hug them.

I peer up at my brothers. We stopped saying it after Mom died, but I really need them to know how I feel. That despite my heart-break over losing Liam, I'm still grateful they're here and they're both equally important to me.

"I love you."

Surprise crosses over Jace's face before he recovers. "Love you, too."

"Damn, baby sis." Cole rolls his eyes. "This amnesia has turned you soft as fuck."

I rip off a piece of the sandwich and throw it at him. "Asshole."

His grin is all teeth. "Yeah, but you love me anyway."

I do.

I take a hearty bite of my food then wipe my mouth with a napkin. "Thank you for—"

"Someone's feeling better today," the nurse chirps from the door-way. She gestures to the wheelchair in front of her. "Feel like going for a stroll in this thing?"

Given I've been confined to a bed for almost six weeks, it sounds like heaven.

I couldn't hold back my smile if I tried. "Absolutely."

I'm so excited about leaving, I attempt to stand up on my own. Unfortunately, my legs feel like spaghetti and I stumble instead.

"Woah," Jace says, rushing to catch me before I bust my ass. "Take it easy, killer."

Cole comes around to the opposite side of me. "You good now, Bambi?"

My mind says yes, but my body vehemently disagrees.

I shake my head. "I can't. It's too soon."

Jace isn't having it. "No, it's not. You got this."

Cole tightens his grip on my arm. "And we got you."

I know.

"Okay," I relent. "Let's do this."

Chapter 9

"*A*re you sure you don't want any hel—"

I close the bathroom door before Sawyer can finish her sentence. It's not that I'm not grateful for her offer to help, I just want to be able to go to the bathroom in peace for once. And thanks to starting physical therapy, I've been upgraded to crutches which means I finally can.

If all goes well, hopefully I'll be discharged soon.

I'm hobbling over to the toilet when I catch my reflection in the mirror and freeze.

Holy shit.

Even though my brain has finally accepted the fact that I'm eighteen and not eight, I haven't given much thought to what I might look like.

"Woah."

Steadying one crutch against the sink, I touch the glass, just to make sure I'm not hallucinating.

Long dark hair, tan skin, big brown eyes, high cheekbones, a slightly upturned nose, and full lips.

The last recollection I have of my appearance, I was the epitome of awkward looking...but now?

Now, I look just like her.

Turning my head ever so slightly, I peer at the scar running down the side of my neck. It's about four inches in length and stops at my collarbone. The fading pink color tells me it must be new.

I vaguely recall the doctor telling me I went through the windshield during the accident and a shard of glass got lodged in my neck, missing my carotid artery by less than a centimeter.

Sucking in a breath, I lift up my shirt, inspecting the scar on my lower abdomen. The one that cost me a kidney thanks to a piece of shrapnel during the accident with my mom. Not only does it appear smaller than I remember, it's faded quite a bit.

But it's still a glaring reminder of the day my mother tried to kill me.

Shoving that thought down and turning my focus to something positive, I raise my shirt higher, checking out the merchandise.

My boobs aren't ginormous or anything, but I'm definitely not disappointed with what mother nature gave me.

I want to examine the rest of my body, but my bladder starts protesting my little peep show so I take care of business before I shuffle back to my hospital room.

I walk in on my dad, brothers, Sawyer, and my doctor having what looks to be a pretty heated discussion.

Oh, boy.

"You're never home," Jace barks at our dad. "There's no way you can take care of her."

As much as I hate hearing them argue, Jace has a point. Amnesia or not, there is one thing I definitively remember most about my father.

His absence.

That said, he's really been stepping up his game lately and has been visiting me a lot.

Dad juts his chin. "I can take some time off work."

Crossing his arms, Jace stares him down. "No. She's staying with me and Dylan at our apartment. This way we can watch over her."

I'm tempted to remind him that I'm not a child, but I know Jace's heart is in the right place and he's only looking out for me.

Dad's visibly irate now. "Last I checked, *I* was the father here, Jace."

Jace snorts. "Only when it's convenient—"

"Stop!" I shout, because I honestly can't stand another second of this.

Everyone turns to look my way.

"Hello, Bianca," Dr. Jones greets me and there's no mistaking the pity in his eyes. "We were just discussing plans for your upcoming discharge."

Normally I'd be happy about the news, but not when it's causing my family to fight like this.

I glare at Dad and Jace. "Can we do it without fighting?"

Sawyer gives me a sympathetic smile. "Bianca's right. Fighting isn't what she needs right now, and it's not going to make anything better. In fact, why don't we ask *her* what she wants and where she'd like to stay."

"Can I stay with you?" I joke, although part of me is being serious.

I know Jace loves Dylan, but something about her rubs me the wrong way and I'm not sure why. Needless to say, the prospect of living with her isn't exactly something I'm looking forward to.

Sawyer looks at Cole. "I mean, we do have a pull-out couch in our apartment."

Cole's brows lift. "Yeah." His eyes meet mine. "You can stay with us if you want—"

"She's staying with me and Dylan," Jace cuts in. "Our apartment has an extra bedroom."

"A bedroom she has absolutely no recollection of ever being in." Dad turns to Dr. Jones. "You said earlier that being in her typical surroundings might help with her amnesia, correct?"

Dr. Jones nods. "Yes, although it doesn't necessarily guarantee she'll get her memory back."

"But being in her own home gives her the best chance of that happening, right?"

Another nod. "It certainly wouldn't be a bad thing."

Dad looks at Jace. "Then it's settled. Bianca's coming home."

Jace grinds his teeth so hard I'm surprised they don't turn into dust. "You sure that's going to be okay with *Nadia*?"

He spits her name out like it's rancid food.

"Nadia?" I repeat, looking between them. "Who's Nadia?"

"Dad's fiancée," Cole mutters, his nose turning up in disgust.

Oh.

"I didn't...I had no idea."

I'm honestly not sure what to say or how I should feel about this.

I mean, I want my dad to be happy and it's been ten years since Mom died, so it's not like I would have expected him to put his love life on hold or anything.

But part of me—a huge part—can't help but feel a pang of overwhelming sadness.

She should be here.

Correction—*they* should be here.

"We got engaged a couple of months ago," Dad explains. "And Nadia isn't living at the house yet. Although I would like her to move in soon so she can help me take care—"

"Over my dead fucking body, old man," Jace growls. "No way in hell am I letting your *mistress* play pretend mom to my baby sister. Besides, you know as well as I do that shit would never fly if Bianca was in her right state of mind."

I can't help but flinch at his words.

Guilt colors Jace's expression. "I'm sorry, I didn't mean it like that. I just…even though you can't remember things, Cole and I do. Trust me, letting Nadia play stepmom isn't something you'd want." He blows out a heavy breath. "I'm just trying to look out for you."

I know he is.

"He's right," Cole adds, backing him up. "You don't trust a lot of people, Bianca." He looks at Dad. "Hell, the only thing *any* of us know about Nadia is that she's the whore you used to sneak out of the house after your little booty call was over."

Well, damn. That was…harsh.

"Colton," Sawyer hisses. "Stop being an asshole."

"Nadia was *never* my booty call, and she's certainly not a whore," Dad seethes. "And the only reason you three don't know anything about my fiancée is because you all refuse to be around her."

As much as it pains me to agree, he has a point. It doesn't really sound like we've made any move to get to know this woman Dad's marrying at all.

Although truth be told, if my choices are living with Jace and Dylan versus Dad and this Nadia woman, I have to go with my gut.

I look at my father. "I wouldn't be opposed to meeting Nadia one day." My stare snags on Jace. "But as long as the offer still stands, I'd prefer to live with you and Dylan."

Living with Jace is way more comfortable than living with a woman I can't recall ever meeting and my dad who I don't know much about either.

Jace smiles. "Good. Because Dylan and I really want you—"

"Hold on," Dad interjects, as if he's pondering something. "How about we compromise?"

I'm game. "Compromise sounds good."

Jace doesn't share my enthusiasm. "What kind of compromise?"

Dad strokes his chin. "There are seven bedrooms at home, which means there is more than enough room for everyone." He looks around at all of us. "Why don't you and Cole move back in?" He clears his throat. "Of course you're welcome to invite Sawyer and Dylan as well."

Jace's nostrils flare. "Are you out of your damn min—"

"It's not a bad idea," I cut in.

Not only do I love the notion of spending more time with my family and Sawyer, being at home might help fix my memory like Dr. Jones said.

Unfortunately, Jace is quick to shut it down. "It's a terrible idea, Bianca. I know you don't remember, but there's a reason I moved out shortly after I graduated high school."

My face falls. "Oh."

My disappointment must be tangible because he sighs. "But I want to give you the best chance for recovery, so I'll do it." He glares at Dad. "Under two conditions."

Dad's sigh is expansive. "What's that?"

"One—I'm doing this for Bianca, not you, so don't think this fixes shit between us. And two—Nadia isn't moving into Mom's house while we're there."

I can tell Dad wants to argue, but he's a smart man and for once puts his children first. "She won't move in until after the wedding. You have my word."

Cole looks at Sawyer. "You down for a temporary address change, Bible Thumper?"

She tugs her lower lip between her teeth. "I don't know."

"Please," I beg, even though I probably have no right to. "I can't remember our friendship, but something tells me I'd really like having you around." I flutter my fingers. "I'll even let you paint my nails."

I feel a closeness to the girl I can't really explain. Plus, she has a really good aura.

At that, she laughs, folding like a cheap lawn chair. "Okay, fine. If you really want me there...I'll do it."

Dropping my crutches, I throw my arms around her. "You're the best."

She freezes briefly before hugging me back. "Oh. Um...this is...nice."

Cole laughs. "Told you she turned soft."

And just like that, the nagging feeling in my gut is back with a vengeance.

Who the hell is Bianca Covington?

Chapter 10

$\mathcal{M}$y eyes are wide as I take everything in. "*This* is my bedroom?"

It's a lot different from what I remember.

Back when I was eight, stuffed animals and dolls filled the large space.

Now it's...books, hair tools, nail polish, makeup, shoes, and what looks like a gigantic walk-in closet.

Darting my gaze around, I can't help but notice the pink three-mirrored vanity in the far corner.

Everything in my room is a various shade of purple. Except that.

"It was Mom's," Cole says as if answering my unspoken question.

That makes sense. Pink was her favorite color.

It used to be mine, too.

As if remembering the happy times, Jace's face lights up. "She loved that thing. I remember the excitement on her face when Dad gifted it to her one year for Christmas. It was an ant—"

"Antique from France," I finish for him as the memory floats through my head. "I used to love watching her apply her lipstick in the morning."

She was always so careful. So precise.

So perfect.

And I wanted nothing more than to be just like her.

Hobbling over to my queen-size bed, I touch the silky purple bedspread.

Ten years ago, I had a comforter with unicorns on it.

Now everything's different.

Even the walls which are now painted purple.

Adjusting my crutches, I stagger over to my closet.

I try to open it, but it's stuck.

"Here," Jace says, handing me a remote.

A remote-controlled door for a *closet*? "Why in the world would I need this?"

Cole barks out a laugh. "You didn't want anyone stealing your clothes."

I can see why the moment it slides open.

Holy shit.

Even to the untrained eye, there's no hiding the fact that everything in here is very expensive and very designer.

It's also *very* skimpy and attention-grabbing.

Well, everything except for the five crisp white button-down shirts and plaid skirts.

"Is that my school uniform?"

I'm really hoping they say yes because they're the only normal outfits in here.

"Yeah," Jace answers. "You ready for your big day tomorrow?"

Not even close.

Evidently, I'm a senior at Royal Hearts Academy.

I was worried I'd have to repeat the year given I missed the first two months of school, but my dad assured me he talked to the principal and as long as I maintain my excellent grades, I'll be allowed to finish the year and graduate with the rest of my class.

Jace and Cole let it slip that *talked to the principal* was code for writing the school a check.

Either way, I'm glad my absence and accident won't impact me graduating on time.

Although I am nervous about having to explain to everyone that I have amnesia.

Surprise roots me to the spot as I take in a blue and white cheerleading skirt, matching top, and a set of pom-poms.

"I'm a cheerleader?"

Just like Mom wanted.

"Nah, little sis. You're the cheerleading *captain*," Cole muses.

I gesture to my crutches. "That might be an issue."

Sadness flickers in Cole's eyes. "Yeah."

"But hey," Jace says. "You were close to the girls on the squad so I'm sure whoever the new captain is will let you hang out with them."

Cole snorts. "Not likely."

"Would you shut up?" Jace mutters. "I'm not trying to scare her."

And here they go talking about me like I'm not even in the room again.

"Why would I be scared?"

"Because Royal Hearts Academy isn't a regular high school," Dylan says from the doorway.

"It's hell on earth," Sawyer adds with a shudder. "The whole place is filled with rich evil spawns whose only talent consists of swiping their parents' credit cards and tossing rude insults to the less fortunate."

Damn. That doesn't sound like someplace I'd want to be at all.

I swallow thickly. "Really?"

Jace blows out a breath. "So much for that."

"Sorry," Sawyer says. "But I'd want to know what I was getting into if I was her." Glancing my way again, Sawyer adds, "I'm sorry for freaking you out." She gestures to my cheerleading uniform. "On the bright side, you're really pretty and popular, so I'm sure you'll be fine."

"She *was* popular," Dylan mutters.

When we all look at her, she shrugs and says, "Bianca has amnesia which means she's at a disadvantage and officially fresh meat to them." She points to herself. "And as someone who was also the newbie during her senior year, I feel it's only fair to give you some advice."

I'm all ears. "What's that?"

"Get some thick skin and don't take any crap from anyone because those vultures are going to hop on you like flies on shit tomorrow."

My stomach churns. "Oh."

"She's a Covington, babe," Jace argues. "No one will mess with her."

Despite his reassuring words, I see apprehension etching his features.

Cole plops down on my bed and sighs. "No one would mess with her if we still went there...but we don't." He looks at Jace. "Which means we can't protect her anymore."

Jesus. They're making this place sound like a damn warzone instead of an educational institution.

"I'll be fine," I assure everyone.

Besides, how bad could it possibly be?

Chapter 11

*J*ace halts me the moment I open the car door. "You need money for lunch."

"Oh…right."

He hands me a fifty-dollar bill. "Here."

I blink. "Uh…this must be lunch money for the month, right?"

"Nope," Dylan says from the passenger seat. "Not if you want a decent meal in this place."

Shooting him a grateful smile, I tuck it into my purse and haul my backpack over my shoulders.

"Thanks for giving me a ride. See you at three."

Grabbing my crutches, I hop to my feet.

As Jace gets out of the car.

"What are you doing?"

He shrugs like it's no big deal. "Walking you inside." Pounding on his chest, he looks around the parking lot that's full of people. "Because *I'm* her big brother. And I will fuck all of you little shit stains up if you mess with her."

Not taking his threat seriously, a few kids nearby start howling with laughter.

"Dude, you went here like forty years ago," some guy calls out. "No one gives a shit about you anymore."

More laughter. *Perfect.*

Heat flushes over my cheeks. I literally want the ground to

swallow me up. Or rather, swallow Jace up so he'd quit embarrassing me.

I look to Dylan for help.

Fortunately, she's quick on the uptake. "Stop it, Jace. Bianca will be fine."

My brother isn't having it though. "I'll be back in a minute."

Dylan crooks a finger at him. "Come here."

When he does, she whispers something in his ear that has his eyes turning dark and hazy with lust.

Yuck.

Jace looks at me. "On second thought, I think you can handle this on your own."

'Thank you,' I mouth to Dylan as Jace hops into the driver's seat.

It seems I was all wrong about her because she's actually pretty cool.

Drawing in a deep breath, I shuffle my way inside the building.

It feels like everyone's eyes are on me the entire time and there's a shit-ton of whispers following in my wake.

Things like, "I thought she died?"

Or, "I can't believe she's back. Caitlyn's going to flip."

And, "Check out that gnarly scar on her neck."

I'm so focused on keeping my head down and not making any waves, I bump right into someone on the way to my locker.

"Watch where you're going, freakshow," some girl chirps.

"Sorry," I mutter to the pretty, slender blonde.

With her flawless makeup and perfectly styled hair, she looks like she belongs on a magazine cover.

I can't help but notice the group of equally pretty girls surrounding her like a pack of wolves.

Ready to pounce.

I eye the blue and white gym bag she's holding. It matches the one I have in my closet. Right next to my cheerleading uniforms and pom-poms.

"Are you a cheerleader?"

If so, these are the girls I'm supposed to be friends with. Although they look the *opposite* of friendly right now.

The girl scrunches her face. "Wow. That accident must have taken all your brain cells too."

People start to gather around us, forming a circle.

"Man, Caitlyn has balls," some guy calls out.

"Come on, Bianca," another guy shouts. "Let her have it."

I don't want to fight. I just want to meet my friends and make it through this school year in peace.

"Caitlyn, right?" My shoulders slump. "Look, I think we got off on the wrong foot. Things are a little foggy for me since I just got out of the hospital and I have amnesia—"

Caitlyn takes a step in my direction, causing me to back up.

"Let's get one thing straight, freak. I don't give a shit about you and neither does anyone else here. As far as we're all concerned, you died in that accident along with your little lesbian lover."

My head swirls.

Died?

Lesbian lover?

"Someone d-died?" I question, not understanding.

Jace and Cole never told me anything about the accident.

Then again, given the way I reacted to Mom and Liam's death, why would they?

My heart folds in on itself.

Another death.

My throat locks up. *I can't breathe.*

"I—uh. I have to go."

I feel like I'm going to be sick.

Correction: I *am* going to be sick.

My stomach lurches as bile works up my esophagus. I need to get to the bathroom before I puke in front of everyone. "Move, please."

"Don't tell *me* to move, cunt," Caitlyn hisses.

Okay, fine. *I'll* move.

Only I can't...because the crew of girls spreads out, blocking me from leaving.

No, no, no. "Please, mo—"

It's too late.

My stomach jerks in one big wave and before I can stop myself, I'm puking my corn flakes all over Caitlyn's shoes.

People start howling with laughter.

"Damn. The bitch is *back*," someone cackles.

"I'm sorry," I say between dry heaves. "I'm so sor—"

She pushes me, but since I'm not too good on my feet yet, I wobble and teeter.

Right before I end up slipping on my own pool of vomit.

"Ew. That's *so* gross," someone whines.

Some girl makes a gagging sound causing everyone to laugh.

"What a train wreck."

No argument here, because that's *exactly* what I feel like right now.

I tried my best to clean up in the bathroom, but there's still a faint vomit stench that lingers in my skirt.

One that everyone can't help but point out whenever I enter a classroom.

It got so bad, I had no choice but to text Jace and ask if he could drop off another uniform for me.

He did, of course, but it did nothing to stop the whispers and snide comments.

I walked in here today wanting so badly to reconnect with my friends and fit in, but I'm officially a social pariah.

I end up spending my lunch in the bathroom because people refused to let me join them at their table.

For someone who was so popular, the old Bianca doesn't seem to have a true friend in sight.

And this new Bianca?

Well, she's downright lonely.

The only thing I can do is apologize to Caitlyn and offer to buy her new shoes.

Hell, maybe she and I—along with the rest of the team—can go on a shopping trip after school.

We can gossip, they can fill me in on everything I've missed since I've been gone, and I can get to know them again.

We were all friends once, so that means they had to have liked me at some point.

I just need to find the right time to approach Caitlyn and the rest of the team so I can hash things out.

Fortunately, I get my chance when they walk into the bathroom.

Tossing the rest of my sandwich out in a nearby trashcan, I cut my gaze to her.

"Look, Caitlyn, I'm really sorry—"

A sharp punch to my cheek has me seeing stars.

Stunned, I cup my now throbbing cheekbone. "What the hell?"

"Lock the door," Caitlyn instructs.

I hear the faint click of the latch and the remaining group of girls form a tight circle around me.

I reach for my crutches that are leaning against the sink, but they're snatched away. "Not so fast, bitch."

I look around at all of them. I'm not sure why they're being so mean to me, but the pure hatred in their eyes tells me whatever happened between us is bad.

Real bad.

"I don't—"

Another sharp punch to my cheek sends my head reeling.

Past...

I clap my hands. "Let's go, bitches!"

Swear to God, these worthless whores couldn't dance their way out of a paper bag.

The routine isn't even that hard.

I press a button on the speaker and music floods the gymnasium. "Again."

A groan of irritation ripples through my chest as I watch Amber turn and shimmy in the wrong direction, bumping straight into Caitlyn.

Of course, this causes a domino effect and sends the rest of the line teetering and swaying like tree branches in a hurricane.

Only way less graceful.

"Oh, for Christ's sake." My hands clench into fists. "You mother-fucking *idiots.*"

I march over to Amber. "Remind me again why the fuck you're

on my team when you're too stupid to know your lefts from your rights. You just ruined the entire formation, dumbass."

"Maybe if you gave her a break it wouldn't have happened," Caitlyn snaps. "We've been practicing for three hours now without so much as a sip of water."

I glare at her. "Oh, you want some water?" Snatching my water bottle off the table, I pour the contents over her head. "How's this?"

Everyone gasps as it soaks her hair and shirt, but I don't care.

I'm so tired of these assholes expecting handouts and free rides.

These bitches have to learn.

The real world isn't fair and the sooner they realize that, the better.

Because if they want to keep their spots on *my* team, they'll have to continuously work their asses off for it, because being a cheerleader is more than a pretty uniform and pom-poms.

Hands on my hips, I walk down the line, giving each of them their daily critique.

"Renee, do you know how to count?"

Confusion colors her face. "Uh, yeah."

"Then why are you consistently a second late on your jumps?"

Clearly embarrassed, she looks down. "I don't know."

"Well, I suggest you figure it the fuck out. Otherwise you'll be standing outside school tomorrow morning wearing a t-shirt that reads, 'I don't know how to count to three because I'm a dumbass.'"

I move down the line. "Courtney, how many times do I have to tell you to point your toes during a toe touch?"

Her lower lip trembles. "I-I'm sorry."

"Yeah, a sorry excuse for a cheerleader." I make a karate chop with my hands. "Toe touches are different than holding your legs in the air while your ugly boyfriend screws you in his shitty truck for forty seconds. Your legs need to be straight and your toes need to be pointed at all times. Don't make me have to tell you again."

Sighing, I move on to the next girl. *Morgan.* She's been a thorn in my side for as long as I've known her and doesn't deserve to be here.

However, she does have a certain *talent.*

Too bad it doesn't involve cheerleading.

It's just one of many reasons why I stole the team captain spot from her.

"I'm not gonna sugarcoat this, heifer. Drop five pounds or I'm dropping your fat ass from the squad." Leaning over, I hiss, "I don't care *what* you offer this time."

Morgan isn't actually fat, but she's not in shape like the rest of us which means her jumps aren't high enough and it's noticeable.

She starts to speak, but I hold up my hand, focusing on the next girl.

The one responsible for sending everyone tumbling earlier. "Amber, give me your right hand."

When she does, I draw the letter R on it with a black Sharpie. Then I draw the letter L on her left.

Maybe this will teach the idiot her rights from her lefts.

Because I'm still so fired up, I write the word *stupid* on her forehead for good measure.

"Don't wash these off until you convince me otherwise. Got it?"

Teary-eyed, she nods.

I move to the last girl. *Caitlyn.*

Last year she actually voted for me to be team captain instead of Morgan, but this year it's like she's determined to fight with me every step of the way.

Fortunately for her, I can't kick her off the squad because she's good.

Really good.

I can, however, put her in her place.

"And *you.* I really hope you're not planning on being a professional cheerleader because the only thing you'll ever be good at is spreading your legs. Just like your gold-digging mother."

Fire flashes in her eyes and I dare her with mine to mouth off because I'll send her packing with her tail between her legs.

I get uncomfortably close to her face. "Got something to say?"

She opens her mouth like she's going to, but thinks better of it.

My smile is wicked. "Smart girl."

I clap my hands and turn the music back on. "Again, humpty dumpties."

Chapter 12

*T*he pain pounding through my skull is so bad my vision becomes blurry.

There are so many kicks and punches coming my way, there's no way I can possibly deflect them all.

The only thing I can do is curl up in a ball on the floor as they continue giving me what I deserve.

No wonder they all hate me so much. *I was downright awful to them.*

Someone leans over me. Amber, I think.

She takes out a Sharpie and begins scribbling something on my forehead.

"I'm sorry."

A bolt of pain shoots through my eye socket. "Shut up."

A scream tears from my throat as someone else snatches a fistful of my hair and another girl plugs my nose.

A moment later liquid fills my mouth. I choke and sputter on the water, trying to get some air into my lungs, but it's no use.

Caitlyn laughs like it's the funniest thing she's ever seen. "Enjoying your water?" She leans in. "What's that? You want some more?"

My lungs burn and white spots form in front of my eyes.

I'm gonna die.

And the worst part is...I can't even fault them for what they're doing.

Because I created this…created them.

Or rather, *she* did.

Finally, the torture ends.

"Tell anyone we did this to you, and it will be ten times worse next time," Amber hisses.

It hurts so bad, I can't even speak.

Caitlyn grabs my crutches. "I'd be nice and give these back, but you're a wicked little bitch who doesn't deserve shit."

She passes my crutches to another girl. "Burn them." Crouching down, she spits in my face. "Don't ever breathe in our direction again, got it?"

Tears spring to my eyes and I nod.

I feel so humiliated, so dejected.

So worthless.

Cackling, Amber snaps a picture of me on her phone. "Oh, how the mighty have fallen."

"They did *what?*" my father booms as he strides into the hospital room.

The same one I was discharged from three days ago.

How's that for irony?

On the upside, most of the damage is in the form of bruises that make my face and body look like a paint by numbers portrait.

Well, apart from the broken rib that throbs with every breath I take.

"They fucking *jumped* her," Jace explains, growing more irate by the second.

"Remind me again what the jail time is for hiring a hitman to take out a group of high school skanks?" Cole grunts.

Sawyer rubs his back. "I knew Bianca wasn't always *pleasant*, but ganging up and jumping her in a bathroom is just…"

"Beyond fucked up." Expression full of disgust, Dylan looks at me. "Want me to give them a taste of their own medicine?"

As much as I appreciate her offer, I don't believe two wrongs make a right.

Something tells me I can't say the same about my former self.

Jace clenches his fists. "We can't let them get away with this."

"We need to call the police." Cole's green eyes flash with rage. "Have those little bitches arrested."

Dad takes out his phone. "Oh, trust me, son, when I'm through with them—"

I quickly halt him before he makes the phone call. "I don't want you to call the police."

As nice as it is to hear them all getting along for once, this isn't what I want.

Five sets of eyes blink in confusion.

Jace looks at me like I've sprouted another head. "Why not?"

I take a deep breath and let it out. "Because I deserved it."

That does nothing to clear up their confusion.

"Bianca," Sawyer says softly. "No one deserves this."

She's wrong. "I'd agree, but while they were…you know, beating me up. I had a flashback." I wipe my damp palms on my skirt. "I— uh. I was *really* mean to them." Tears clog my vision because I feel like such a horrible person. "I made their lives miserable and I think they attacked me today to protect themselves and make sure I knew they wouldn't stand for it anymore."

And I can't blame them one iota.

Sawyer and Dylan exchange a glance.

The fact that no one jumps to my defense tells me all I need to know.

The old Bianca was rotten to the core.

Unfortunately for me, I'm the one paying for her behavior.

My stomach rolls with my next thought. God only knows how many enemies I have at school.

Finally, Jace speaks, "Bianca, I get what you're saying, but we still have to do something. What they did was…extreme."

Cole nods in agreement. "I don't care how much of a bitch you were to them in the past, it doesn't warrant them attacking you the way they did. For fuck's sake, you need crutches to get around. You couldn't defend yourself even if you wanted to."

"Which is exactly why they did it," Dylan whispers, appearing deep in thought. "They wanted to strike while she was down."

Sawyer huffs out an irritated breath. "Which means this wasn't an impulsive mistake that got out of hand." Her face scrunches up. "It was calculated."

Cole rubs his forehead. "Man, who knew girls could be so damn vindictive."

Sawyer and Dylan give him a look as if to say, '*Duh.*'

Dad holds up his phone. "I'm going to have them all arrested for assault and put behind bars." Sadness flickers in his eyes. "Sweetheart, I know I haven't always…" His voice trails off and he tries again. "I need to make sure you're safe and those girls pay for what they did to you."

Jace's expression softens and for once he's not looking at our father like he's dirt on the bottom of his shoes.

"Hold on," I say as the thought occurs to me. "I think I have a better solution."

If Caitlyn and the rest of the cheerleaders want me gone and the entire school has a preconceived notion of me because of how I was…maybe, it's best I go someplace new.

This way, *this* Bianca can have a fresh start and not be judged for what she did and how she treated people in the past.

"I want to change schools."

Jace and Dad exchange a perplexed glance.

"Why?" Cole questions. "All your friend—" I can see the exact moment it dawns on him. "Right."

Dad shakes his head. "Absolutely not. Royal Hearts Academy is a very prestigious school. One that looks spectacular on college applications. I'm not letting these girls ruin your future."

Jace shrugs. "Plus, the only school you'd be able to transfer to is Royal Manor High."

"And trust me, you *don't* want to go there. That place is full of gangs and thugs from the bad side of town." Cole narrows his eyes. "Not to mention their football team sucks balls."

It's all I can do not to roll my eyes.

"I was at RHA for four hours and got jumped in the bathroom," I remind them. "Besides, going someplace new would give me a fresh start—"

"No," Dad argues. "It's out of the question."

Agitated, I fall against the hospital bed. It's clear he's not going to budge without a fight, and I've had enough fighting for one day.

"I still don't want them arrested—" I start to say until I remember something Caitlyn said to me. "The accident…"

I can't even bring myself to say the words.

Jace's brows pinch. "What's wrong?"

The muscles in my back tighten as I force in a shaky breath. "Did someone die?"

Jace exhales sharply and takes a step in my direction, approaching me like I'm a bomb that's about to go off at any minute. "Where did you hear that?"

I tell him the truth. "Caitlyn. She said my…" I pause because I'm still trying to wrap my head around it. Then again, nothing about my former life surprises me anymore, so I guess it's not entirely out of the question. "She said my lesbian lover died in the accident."

Needless to say, everyone is speechless.

Including me, because I don't recall *anything* about this girl.

Jace clamps his mouth shut, like he's trying to decide the right words to say.

I look to Cole for answers, but he's locked up tight too.

I try Sawyer next, but she looks down at her feet.

"Can *someone* please tell me what happened."

"We don't really know," Jace responds after another minute passes. "We weren't there."

Understandable, but they still have to know more than I do. "But you all know what happened after, right?" I press a hand to my quivering belly. "Did she…did she die?"

Lines strain along Cole's mouth, like he's trying his hardest not to speak. I silently plead with him to tell me the truth because after pretending to be Liam, he owes me that much.

"Hayley didn't make it," he finally whispers.

Despite the fact that the name isn't one I can recall, my heart spirals with grief.

Another death.

I'm starting to feel like there's a bad omen over my head and whoever I love is destined to meet the grim reaper.

"Oh, my God."

My head whirls. *I can't take it anymore.*

"I know everything sucks right now," Jace says, pulling me close. "But we're all here for you."

For how long?

How long before they end up dead too?

I don't even bother wiping my tears away.

I just let them fall.

What's the point of living when everyone I care about dies?

Jace looks at our dad. "On second thought, maybe a fresh start isn't such a bad idea."

Dad's expression is solemn. "I'll take care of it."

Chapter 13

*I*f I thought Jace was overprotective dropping me off at RHA for my first day, it's nothing compared to the way he is when he drops me off at Royal Manor High.

Only this time, he's not with Dylan.

He's with Cole.

And the both of them are driving me nuts.

"Don't talk to *anyone*," Jace says. "I don't care if they seem nice."

I want to remind him that it will be hard for me to make new friends that way, but then Cole says, "If anyone offers you drugs, don't take them."

Good grief. *They can't be serious.*

"Say no to drugs," I mutter. "Got it."

"If someone tries to get you someplace alone," Jace grunts, his hand tightening around the steering wheel. "Run away because it's a trap."

"But not before kicking them in the balls." Cole flicks his gaze to me. "Because you never know. They could be sex trafficking."

My mouth drops open. "Are you two *done* yet?"

Jace pulls into an empty spot and cuts the engine. "No." He turns around to face me. "I got you something."

"What?"

He pulls a metal object out of his pocket. A second later a small blade pops up.

I glare at him in disbelief. "You got me a knife?"

"A pocket knife," he corrects. "Keep it on you for protection."

I look around. Aside from everyone being dressed in regular street clothes and the faint sound of rap music blaring in the distance, it looks *exactly* like the Royal Hearts Academy parking lot.

Ergo, I'm no less safe here than I was there.

I adjust my backpack and grab my crutches. "I'm not carrying a knife."

Not taking no for an answer, Jace slips it into my purse. "Just in case."

Because I know there's no point arguing with him when he's like this, I open the car door and step out.

"Want me to walk you—"

"No," I snap, cutting him off. "I'll be fine."

Because *no one* knows the old Bianca here.

I slam the door with my crutch. "Thanks for the ride."

Cole sticks his head out the passenger side window. "Remember, if anyone messes with you, punch them in the crotch and call us."

"Got it." I flutter my fingers. "Buh-bye."

It's not that I'm not appreciative, I just need a little breathing room.

They make no motion to leave, which no doubt means they're going to watch me walk inside.

Sighing, I adjust my crutches and start hobbling across the parking lot.

I glance around. If I thought *my* closet was full of revealing clothing, it's nothing compared to what some of these girls are wearing.

There's so much bare skin, I feel out of place in my jeans and the t-shirt I borrowed from Dylan.

I'm so focused on everyone else instead of where I'm walking, I slam into someone as I enter the building.

"Watch it, slut," some girl sneers.

I take in her thin frame, long curly brown hair, dramatic makeup, and pointy talons that seem to go on forever.

The girl looks like she can easily kick my ass from here all the way back to the other side of town if she wanted to.

"Sorry."

She gets uncomfortably close to my face. "You should be."

I want to scream because it seems like no matter what high school I attend, there's always a Queen B.

I notice the small group of girls behind her. *And her minions.*

"Come on, Mercedes," one of them urges. "Kick her ass already so we can go."

The girl—who I assume must be Mercedes—smiles smugly as she appraises me from head to toe. "Looks like someone already did."

Yup, and I'm *not* in the mood for a repeat performance.

"Look, I really don't want any problems." I gesture to the paper in my hand. "I just want to find my locker."

Before I can stop her, she yanks the paper from my hand and scans it.

Her eyes darken before they narrow.

I'm about to ask what the problem is, but she rips the paper to shreds and shoves past me.

Awesome.

♕

"*I*f you have any questions or concerns, I want you to feel free to come straight to me," Mrs. Rodriguez—the principal—tells me.

The second I walked into the office for a new schedule, she called me inside hers.

And she's been talking non-stop ever since.

"Thanks." I glance at the clock. Homeroom is going to end any minute. "I should probably get going."

"Not so fast, I'm still waiting on your student pal."

"My student pal?"

I have no idea what that is.

"Yes." She wipes crumbs of donut off her mouth and licks her finger. "Your father told me about your unique circumstances, and I felt the best thing to do was to set you up with someone from the Peer Assistance Program. This way, you'll have someone to walk you to all your classes for the first few days and show you around."

"Oh." All things considered; it doesn't sound like a terrible idea. "Thank—"

She looks past me. "Here he is now." Frantically, she waves her hands. "Hey, Stone, come on in. I'd like you to meet Bianca Covington."

Stone hovers around five-ten, with a slim build, short jet-black hair, a chiseled jaw, and well…a very attractive face.

However, it's the anger harboring in his dark brown eyes that suck all the oxygen out of the room.

I have no idea who he is, but the venom behind his stare is unnerving.

"Hi." I hold out my hand, hoping to make nice. "I'm Bianca."

"Fuck off."

Well, then.

Mrs. Rodriguez nearly chokes on her donut. "Stone, is there a problem?"

"Yeah, there is. I'm sorry, Mrs. Rodriguez, but you're gonna need to find someone else. I can't—"

"Why?" I interject. "Why can't you show me around?"

The anger in those brown orbs kicks up a notch. "You've got to be kidding me."

Does he know me? Because it sure seems like he does.

And if that's the case, I need to know what I did to piss him off because I don't want to face another situation like the one at RHA.

"Look, I don't know what I did to upset yo—"

"Jesus Christ." His jaw works. "You're a real piece of work."

With that, he hightails it out of the office.

"I'm so sorry. He's never been like thi—" Mrs. Rodriguez starts to say, but I'm already chasing after him.

Well, as much as I can with my crutches.

"Stone, wait," I call out. "Please."

He keeps walking.

"Look, I'm sorry for whatever I might have done to you."

That has him turning around. "Seriously?"

I blink. "Yes?"

Grimacing, he leans in. "All right, cut the shit. What the fuck are you really doing here?"

Drawing in a deep breath, I tell him the truth. "A couple of months ago, I was in a car accident and in addition to a broken pelvis, I have amnesia. I can only remember little bits and pieces of my life and those bits and pieces come at random. I used to attend Royal Hearts Academy, but apparently I pissed off a bunch of people there and—" I point to my still bruised face and black eye. "This was the result."

There. It's all out in the open.

He starts howling with laughter. "Man, I always knew you were batshit, but *this*?" He holds up his hands. "This is on a whole new level."

To say I'm confused would be an understatement. "Batshit?"

"Yeah." He swirls his finger around his ear. "Batshit *crazy*."

"I know what batshit means, I'm just trying to figure out why...or rather, *what* I did to make you feel that way about me."

Leaning against a locker, he studies my face for what feels like an eternity. "You're shitting me, right?"

I pinch the bridge of my nose. "No, I'm not *shitting* you."

His tongue finds his cheek. "Well, for starters, how about the time you photoshopped a baby dick onto my body and then spread it around like herpes to our entire freshman class?"

I wince.

Bianca sure stirred up a lot of shit.

He starts ticking things off with his fingers. "There was also the time you and your brother showed up at my job and assaulted my boss—who you spread lies about by the way—before your brother beat the fuck out of me for no reason."

Well, shit. "Oh."

"Yeah, *oh*." He pulls a face. "And I still haven't forgotten that night at the marina—" He averts his gaze. "On second thought, that's not important. All that matters is that it also resulted in Cole attacking me once *again* at my job."

The hurt look on his face tells me whatever happened that night *does* in fact matter. "What happened at the marina?"

A muscle in his jaw bunches. "Don't play dumb, Bianca." A threatening look enters his eyes as he leans in. "Last, but not least, let's not forget the fact that you and your psycho family ruined my brother's life."

"Ruined your brother's life?" I repeat, not understanding. "How?"

He laughs, but there's not a drop of humor. "You know he had nothing to do with Liam's—"

My heart twists at the mention of my brother's name. "You knew Liam?"

I have no idea what to make of the expression on his face. "Well, no. I didn't, but Tommy did."

Tommy.

Hurt is a potent throb in my temples. I feel like something is trying to break through the surface, but it can't.

"Stone?"

"What?" he snarls.

"How did my family ruin your brother's life? And what did Liam have to do with it?"

Stone tilts his head as if trying to view me from a new angle. Whatever he sees has his expression softening. "You really don't remember, do you?"

I give my head a shake. "No. Like I said, I have amnesia."

With a sigh, he snatches the paper out of my hand and examines it. "Go fucking figure."

"What?"

"Not only do we have the same English class first period, our lockers are next to each other."

"Oh." My teeth snag on my lower lip. "Look, I know you're supposed to hate me for what my family did to your brother, but do you think you can find it in your heart to show me where our lockers are and maybe a class or two?" I shrug helplessly. "I'm confused enough as it is and—"

"I'll help you out." His nostrils flare on an indrawn breath. "On two conditions."

"What?"

"One—don't ask me questions about our past, because it only pisses me off and reminds me why I shouldn't be helping you to begin with. And two—after today, promise you'll stay the hell away from me."

I don't like the sound of that at all, but what other choice do I have? "Sure thing."

He juts his chin. "Your locker is down here, Bourne."

I blink. "Bourne?"

He looks at me like I'm a Martian. "Jason Bourne."

That doesn't make anything clearer. "Am I supposed to know who that is?"

"*Bourne Identity.*"

Still drawing a blank. "Is that like a video game or something?"

He laughs, and this time, it's genuine. "You've never seen the Bourne films?"

"Maybe." I shrug. "I have no idea."

"Right." He snorts as we stop short in front of my locker. "The irony."

I turn the lock to the correct combination, and it jerks open. However, there's no way to swing my bookbag off and maintain my balance at the same time. Not when I'm still relying on my crutches for support.

Fortunately, Stone comes to my rescue and slides my backpack off my shoulders for me.

A tingle zips up my spine the second we make contact. "Thanks."

My palms turn sweaty and I'm positive I'm blushing.

Luckily, Stone doesn't seem to notice because he's glancing at his watch. "We're late for class."

Class is the least of my worries right now.

Stone drops a tray of food in front of me. "Enjoy."

I inspect the unappealing grayish meat and dollop of mashed potatoes. It's definitely nothing like the lunches they serve at Royal Hearts Academy. "I appreciate it, but I could have gotten it myself."

He eyes my crutches as he takes a seat across from me. "Really?"

He has a point.

Picking up my fork, I opt for the safer of the two choices and dig into the potatoes. They taste like they're made out of cardboard. "These are...*interesting.*"

He shovels his forkful of meat into his mouth. "Sorry it's not up to par, princess. Maybe you should go back to your rich, fancy private school."

His words hurt.

But not nearly as much as hearing him reduce me to nothing more than a spoiled princess.

I look down at my plate. "You don't even know me."

Hell, *I* don't even know me.

For a brief moment something flashes in his eyes before they turn hard. "Oh, but I do."

I want to argue with him, but I notice a group of girls approaching our table in my peripheral.

"Can we talk for a minute?" the girl who tore up my schedule this morning asks Stone.

I expect him to oblige, but he doesn't. In fact, he looks downright annoyed with her being here. "I already told you, Mercedes. We have *nothing* to talk about."

Mercedes doesn't look like she cares for that answer one bit, however it's *me* she takes her irritation out on.

Leaning over, she slams her hand down on the table. "Guess you found yourself a new *puta*, huh?"

I've been learning new things about myself every day. Today I learned that I know some Spanish.

And that I've had enough of people's shit. "First off—I'm not a slut. Secondly, you really shouldn't talk about yourself that way."

Stone's lips twitch in amusement.

Mercedes coils her head like a snake. "Excuse me?"

Steepling my fingers, I calmly explain it to her. "You said Stone found himself a new puta. Therefore, one can only deduce that you must have been his *first* puta." Picking up my fork, I swallow a bite of potatoes. "Like I said, you really shouldn't talk about yourself that way."

Or me.

"Oh, shit," one of her minions jeer. "You gonna let her disrespect you like that, Mercedes?"

Why, oh, why does every mean girl seem to have an asshole side-kick egging her on all the time?

"Hell naw." Mercedes looks like she wants to strangle me. "I ain't no one's puta, cunt."

"I wasn't the one who said you were," I remind her. "*You* did."

It's clear our little verbal sparring is too much for her to handle.

"Bitch, I'm gonna fuck you up."

She lunges for me, but Stone stands, putting himself between us. "I have some time before work today. Meet me in the parking lot after school."

This seems to calm her down a little. "Yeah, okay." She turns her furious gaze on me. "This ain't over, puta."

My smile is all teeth. "For the last time, I'm *not* a pu—"

"Bianca?"

I look at Stone. "Yeah?"

"She's leaving. Let it go."

"Right."

Mercedes and her crew stalk off and Stone plops back down in his seat.

"How long did you two date?"

He freezes. "What makes you think we dated?"

He's got to be kidding me.

"I might not remember most things, but I'm smart enough to know that when a girl acts like *that*, it's because she's jealous."

He stabs his mystery meat with his fork. "Five months." He takes a bite and wipes his mouth with a napkin. "I ended things with her a few weeks ago."

There's a weird flicker of disappointment in my chest.

"Five months is like an eternity in high school. You must have really cared about her."

"Yeah." He clears his throat. "But walking in on her fucking my brother when he was visiting last month put an end to that."

Wow. Sometimes there just aren't any words.

"I...uh. I'm sorry."

"Don't be." Shrugging, he twists open the bottle of his sports drink. "Like Tommy said, at least I found out she wasn't loyal before things got even more serious between us."

I want to point out that Tommy doesn't sound very *loyal* either, but it's obvious he's pretty close to his brother.

Given I'm close to mine, I can't fault him for that.

He sighs. "Can we talk about something else though? Talking about my cheating ex is ruining my appetite."

Understandable.

"Sure." Searching my brain for small talk, I say, "Have you decided what college you want to attend?"

His face lights up like the Fourth of July. "It's a long shot, but I'm hoping to get into the pre-med program at Duke's Heart."

Well, *damn*. "Pre-med, huh? That's—"

He cuts me off with a roll of his eyes. "Save it, princess. I'm well aware that not too many poor people like me end up becoming doctors. Like I said, it's a long shot."

"I was going to say that's *awesome*."

He narrows his eyes as if he's expecting me to say something else. "And?"

"And what?"

Assessing me, he leans back in his seat. "Come on, you're not gonna make a joke about me not having to worry because I'm half Asian and therefore must be *super* smart?"

I honestly have no idea what to say to that.

Actually, I do.

"I'm not gonna make a *racist* joke, because racist jokes are never funny. Secondly, I don't judge people or their intelligence based on their race or ethnicity. And I sure as hell hope no one judges me based on mine."

Although some people do unfortunately.

My mind flits back to the time Mom took Liam and me to the mall and one woman yelled that she and her ingrate kids should go back to India because we weren't wanted here.

My mom was proud of being Indian and wanted us to be proud of it too. Seeing the crushed look on her face just about killed me.

There was also the time in second grade where we were supposed to give a presentation on our family trees and where we came from, and one of my friends suggested that I focus on my dad's side from Ireland instead of my mom's because people would make fun of me.

People can be such dicks.

Guilt colors Stone's expression. "I'm sorry. I guess you out of all people know what it's like."

"Yeah."

An uncomfortable silence stretches between us for what feels like forever.

"I know you think you know me, Stone, but..." I pause trying, but ultimately failing to find the right words to convey how I feel.

"But what?" he urges.

I push my half-eaten tray of food away. "I guess I'm just hoping you'll give me a chance to show you the new Bianca, because I could really use a friend."

Chapter 14

"*Y*ou were quiet on the car ride home," Jace notes as we walk through the front door. "How was class?"

"Oh, you know…fine."

Given Jace and Cole are overprotective enough already, I'm definitely not going to tell him about Stone DaSilva.

My heart does a little flip. Despite only promising to help me for one day, he walked me to my classes and ate lunch with me again today.

I'd be lying if I said I didn't enjoy our time together.

Or that he wasn't impossibly cute.

Angling my crutches on the staircase, I proceed the long hobble up to my room.

"Woah," Cole calls out as he passes me on the staircase. "Where's the fire?"

Shit. "No fire." I fake a yawn. "I'm just tired."

And by *tired*, I mean I want to go upstairs and do a little digging.

Which reminds me.

"Jace?"

"Yeah?"

"Were you able to fix my laptop?"

Evidently, it has some kind of virus. Fortunately, computers are Jace's specialty and he's fixing it for me.

He shakes his head. "Not yet. Still working on it."

Damn.

"I should have it back to you by the end of the night, though."

"Thanks."

With that, I continue my long-winded journey up the stairs.

I breathe a sigh of relief the moment I enter my room…but the moment is short-lived because I hear a knock on my door.

I open it, intending to demand that my brothers give me some space, but to my surprise it's Sawyer on the other side.

"Hi."

I raise an eyebrow. "Hi."

"Want to hang out?" Sawyer gestures to the plate of brownies she's holding. "I come bearing gifts."

Yeah, she did. And they smell fantastic.

"With an offer like that, how can I say no?" I gesture for her to come inside. "Come on in."

After leaning my crutches against my nightstand, I plop down on my bed and gesture for the plate of goodies.

I know Jace and Cole said I was a health food nut before the accident, but I just don't understand how anyone can live without chocolate.

Sawyer hands it over. "They have chocolate chips in them."

It's like music to my ears. "You're a goddess."

Laughing, Sawyer sits down on my bed. "So, make any new friends yet?"

I freeze, debating whether or not I should tell her about Stone. I know we were friends before, but this whole thing is so new to me.

Plus, there's the fact that my family apparently ruined his brother's life and all.

God, I'm so sick of all this drama.

"Um…kind of."

She studies my face. "Kind of?"

Good Lord, it's like she can see right through me.

"Okay, fine. It's a boy," I blurt out. "Quit drilling me, lady."

Her lips twitch. "No pressure to spill, I promise." Her smile is genuine. "For what it's worth, I'm happy for you."

"Don't be." I sigh heavily. "He's amazing and awesome, and nice when he wants to be, but he has a crazy ex-girlfriend named Mercedes who wants to kick my ass every time she sees me." I crinkle my nose. "Oh, and apparently Jace and Cole hate him, so the chances of us being anything more than frenemies is non-existent."

I love my brothers, but sometimes they ruin *everything*.

Confusion spreads across her face. "Why in the world would Jace and Cole hate him?"

I pick at my brownie. "I'm not sure, but it has something to do with his brother." I inwardly groan. "Evidently, we ruined his life which isn't fair because Stone is—"

"Stone?" Sawyer all but squeaks out. "Stone *DaSilva?*"

I nearly choke on my food. "You know him?"

She gets off the bed and begins pacing. "Well, yeah, He...uh... he's a dishwasher, busboy, and part-time hostess at Cluck You."

Small world. "Then you know how cute and awesome he is."

He's also a hard worker from the sounds of it.

"Sure."

A smile touches my lips. Given they're co-workers, I can ask her a bunch of questions about him.

Her pacing picks up speed. "Dammit, of *all* the things."

It doesn't take a genius to figure out that she's privy to something I'm not.

"Sawyer?"

"Yeah?"

"What's going on?"

She stops pacing and looks at me. "Did you say Jace and Cole ruined *his* brother's life?"

"Yeah. That's what Stone said."

She flinches. "Yeah, that's not..." She holds up a finger. "I'll be right back. Don't go anywhere."

I eye her warily as she heads for the door. "Okay."

A moment later she returns with an equally confused Dylan in tow. "What's going on?"

Placing a finger over her lips, Sawyer closes the door. "Houston, we have a problem."

Dylan looks at me. "What kind of problem?"

I shrug. "Beats me."

All I did was tell her about a boy I like at school. I'm not really sure why she's being so extra about everything.

Sawyer drops her voice to a whisper. "Are Cole and Jace still home?"

"No," Dylan says. "They went to the gym." Her nose crinkles. "Can you tell me what's—"

"Bianca has a crush on Stone DaSilva."

Dylan's mouth drops open. "I'm sorry...*what?*"

"Hey," I snap. "I told you that in confidence."

Sawyer bows her head. "I know and normally I wouldn't ever betray your trust, but this is a really big deal. Especially since Stone has you believing Cole and Jace ruined his brother's life."

Dylan's eyes narrow into tiny slits. "Oh, that no-good, rotten son-of-a-bitch—"

"Okay, that's it." Making a fist, I punch my mattress. "Someone better spill the beans."

I'm so tired of being kept in the dark about everything.

Dylan pinches the bridge of her nose. "I'm not sure why that little asshole told you that, but Jace and Cole didn't ruin *his* brother's life." She sucks in a breath. "Tommy basically made it his mission to ruin *Liam's* life."

I feel like I was dunked in a vat of ice water. "What? How?"

Dylan takes a seat on my bed. "Tommy tormented Liam. Every day he would make fun of his stutter and scars and tease him with that ridiculous nickname."

"What nickname?"

"History," she whispers, her voice sounding every bit as shattered as I feel. "Because history always repeats itself."

My stomach churns with the sudden rush of memories. "Liam used to come home with tears in his eyes."

It broke my heart to see him so upset.

I literally wanted to *kill* Tommy for hurting him.

Dylan nods solemnly. "I know."

"That's not all he did," Sawyer notes.

Dylan glares at Sawyer. "Jace doesn't want us—"

"I know, but she has a right to know what happened that night."

She's right.

I look at them both. "Tell me everything."

Chapter 15

I'm going to kill him.

Stone was right, we did ruin Tommy's life…but only because he ruined Liam's *first.*

A shudder runs through me when I think of all the vicious, cruel things he did to him.

Especially the night before his death.

I clutch a hand to my chest. *Liam never told me.*

Just like most of his pain, he kept it hidden deep down.

He didn't give me a chance to save him.

My insides twist with rage. The fact that I was starting to have feelings for someone who could stand there and defend such a vile, *evil* person makes me want to wash my heart out with bleach.

Which is exactly why I took an Uber to Cluck You shortly after kicking Sawyer and Dylan out of my room.

I want to confront the asshole to his face.

I'm downright shivering with adrenaline as I march into Stone's job.

It takes me all of two seconds to spot him standing at the counter.

I don't think, I just act.

Balancing on my crutches, I pick up the nearest object and fling it at him. "You asshole."

Stone ducks in the nick of time, narrowly missing the napkin dispenser I launched at his head. "Jesus Christ. What the hell is the matter with you?"

"*You*. You lied to me, Stone. You looked me right in the eyes and *lied*." I hate the way my voice quivers, but I have no control over it. "I thought we were friends. I thought——"

"Bianca, that's enough," Sawyer calls out, rushing inside the building. "I know you're upset, but this isn't the time or place."

Stone snorts. "Should have known they'd get to you sooner or later."

I open my mouth to tell him off, but a short older man waving a broom yells, "*You*. I told you never to come here again."

I have no idea what he's talking about.

"Relax, Mr. Gonzales," Sawyer says. "She was just leaving."

Ha. Fat chance. "No, I wasn't."

He jabs a finger in my face. "Leave now, or I'll call the police."

"Call them," I bite out.

Stone takes off his apron and throws it on the counter. "I'm taking my ten-minute break."

Mr. Gonzales throws his hands up. "No. No break for you. You cause that mean girl to come in here and ruin my business again!"

Again?

Stone looks at Sawyer. "Cover for me?"

Sawyer is visibly outraged. "Are you out of your *damn* mind?"

"Please," he insists. "I need to talk to Bianca." He folds his arms. "Besides, you owe me for never pressing charges against your boyfriend."

She points to her engagement ring. "Fiancé." Even though it's clear she doesn't want to, she relents. "And fine, you can talk to her, but I swear to God if you upset her, I *will* hurt you."

It's an idle threat since Sawyer wouldn't hurt a fly, but I appreciate the sentiment.

Stone gestures for me to follow him out back.

Once we're outside, I unleash every bit of my pent-up anger on him.

"Tommy bullied Liam every day of his life. He made fun of his stutter, his scars." My pain is a tangible thing, gripping me by the throat. "The night before he died, he tricked Liam into going into a closet so he could see Dylan—the girl he was in love with—make out with his brother. And if that wasn't bad enough, he pointed and laughed at his tears after they walked back inside the gymnasium."

I have to press a hand to my stomach because I feel sick. So fucking sick. "Then he pulled down his pants in front of all their classmates and made fun of his penis."

Tears are streaming down my face now. I can't imagine how humiliated Liam felt at that moment. It makes sense now why I did what I did to Stone. I wanted Tommy to experience what it was like to put a target on your brother's back for no reason and not be able to do anything about it.

"How could you stand there and defend someone so malicious? So *evil*."

"Because he's my brother," Stone roars. "My dad's been in jail since I was eight and Tommy pretty much raised me." He snorts. "Besides, *you're* one to talk, princess. Your brothers aren't exactly upstanding people, either. Believe me, they've done their fair share of terrorizing."

Huge difference. My brothers would never pick on someone the way Tommy picked on Liam. "My brothers would *never*—"

"Oh, yeah?" Stone argues, taking a step in my direction. "Fine, let's talk about all the shit they've done to people."

"What—"

"Shortly after Liam died, Jace hunted him down in the woods and threatened to rape him with a bat right before he killed him. Tommy had to beg and plead for him to spare his life. Not that he had much of a life after that because *everyone* blamed him for Liam's suicide, and he had to change schools." Eyes narrowing, he continues, "When Dylan came back to town, Jace put up posters of her father's mugshot all over school." His jaw tics. "And your brother Cole? Well, in addition to beating me up *twice*, he called Sawyer fat in front of their classmates and made her feel so bad about herself she became addicted to Adderall to lose weight and almost *died*."

I feel sick for a whole new reason now. "How do you know all this?"

"Because when the Covingtons do shit, *everyone* in town talks about it." His smile is vicious. "You want to judge and call me a terrible person for defending my brother, but you're no different, princess."

That may be true. However, Liam's my line you don't cross. *Ever.*

"He was a good person," I whisper.

"Are you fucking *kidding*—"

"Liam," I choke out. "*Liam* was a good person. More than good. He was kind and gentle. Compassionate. He didn't deserve the torture Tommy inflicted on him." I look him right in the eyes. "And I can't be friends with someone who can't see that."

I won't. *No matter how much it might hurt.*

I don't know what to make of the expression on his face. "Duly noted."

Even though my family didn't start this war, I'm ending it.

I have to.

"I guess this is goodbye then."

Go figure. The only friend I made is the one I can't keep.

He starts to walk inside but stops. "Bianca?"

"Wha—"

Soft lips crash against mine in a tender kiss that sizzles all the way from my head to my toes.

"What are you doing?" I whisper against his mouth.

With sad eyes, he pulls away. "Saying goodbye."

Chapter 16

$\mathcal{I}$ scan the restaurant for Sawyer, intending to ask her for a
ride so I can go home and think about what I did.

Correction, what *he* did.

I can't believe Stone kissed me.

And worst of all...I liked it.

Really liked it.

My stomach drops when I spot Sawyer having what looks like a
heated argument with her boss.

Not wanting Mr. Gonzales to see me and threaten to kick me out
again, I hobble my way to the restroom.

I can still feel his kiss lingering on my lips.

Smacking my head, I will myself to stop thinking about it.

Stone and I can't ever be anything more than enemies.

It would be a betrayal to Liam.

Stone isn't Tommy—my mind argues.

I shake the thought out of my head. "Stupid, stupid, stupid."

I'm about to text Sawyer and let her know where I'm hiding out,
but the door swings open.

"Oh, my God. It *is* you."

I take in her chin-length blonde hair, brown eyes, and tall frame.

I have no idea who this girl is.

I tilt my head to the side, studying her. On second thought, she
does look vaguely familiar. I just can't seem to place her.

"God, I'm *so* happy you're okay."

Next thing I know, her arms are wrapped around me, and my crutches are falling to the floor.

I'm surprised for two reasons. One—this is the first person outside of my family who seems legitimately happy to see me after the accident.

And two—apparently, I *do* have a friend.

She cups my face in her hands. "I know the last time we saw each other you said it was over, but—"

Her lips crash against mine.

What. The. *Actual*. Fuck.

Is today everyone kiss Bianca and mess with her head day?

I promptly pull away. "I'm sorry, who are you?"

"Very funny," she coos, her mouth finding my neck.

Past...

J situate myself on the hood of her car and gesture to the cheerleading uniform I'm wearing. "If you want a spot back on the team, you're gonna have to earn it."

Morgan turns white as a sheet. "How?"

It's all I can do not to laugh. The girl has been a thorn in my side since last year. Between making fun of me every chance she got, constantly threatening to kick me off the team once she became the official captain...and *other* things, it was enough to make me want to contemplate dumping her in a vat of sulfuric acid.

But now the tides have turned, and little by little, I'm taking everything away from her.

Her position as cheerleading captain.

Her friends.

Her popularity.

And by the end of tonight...I'll have every ounce of her dignity, too.

Anger mixed with jealousy flows through my veins.

There's only one thing she has that I want.

Of course, it's the one and only thing I can't have.

For now.

Lying back against the windshield, I spread my legs. "By proving your loyalty to me."

I'm not expecting her to actually do it.

No, this is all just part of my little game of fucking with her head.

The CIA has nothing on my forms of torture.

She blinks. "What do you want me to do?"

Fucking idiot. Of course, I'd have to spell it out for her. "Lick my pussy, bitch."

A smile stretches across my face as I wait for her to decline so I can tell her she'll never be on my squad and to enjoy her new *loser* social status.

Morgan chews her bottom lip, her eyes scanning around the empty marina. "Here?"

Hmm. Not the answer I was expecting, but I indulge her because if I'm the one to fold, this will all be for naught.

"Yup." Hooking my thumbs onto the sides of my panties, I slide them off. "Right he—"

A jolt of pleasure mixed with shock runs through me as she lowers her head and begins licking my cunt like a decadent dessert.

Holy shit.

Not many things surprise me anymore, but this certainly does.

A breath leaves me in one big rush as she continues lapping at me.

Damn...she's good.

Too fucking good.

There's no way this is her first time carpet munching.

Grabbing the back of her head, I force her to look at me. "You enjoy eating pussy, don't you?"

Her hooded eyes and the way her tongue comes out for another taste tells me all I need to know.

Ironic given her father is a rich senator who openly hates gay people.

Pleasure sizzles up my spine as her hot mouth suctions around my clit. "Fuck. Just like that."

She moans, her movements picking up speed and I swear I see stars.

Jesus Christ. She's so fucking *good*.

"Oh, God," I gasp, writhing against her face. "On second thought, maybe we can work something out."

Unlike Morgan, I'm not into girls, but I have no problem offering my pussy up for her to dine on from time to time.

Because at the end of the day, it doesn't matter whose mouth is responsible for it, an orgasm is still an orgasm.

That said, I'm not dumb enough not to take the opportunity to score a little blackmail for safekeeping.

Reaching for my phone, I press the record button.

That's when I notice movement out of the corner of my eye.

My stomach clenches as I take in a dark, shadowy figure watching us.

With a phone in his hand.

It occurs to me that I have two options.

I can make Morgan stop and send her home.

However, if I do that it will no doubt alert our little stalker that I'm on to him and give him the opportunity to book it.

Therefore, I'm better off letting her finish me off before I confront him.

Reaching down, I grab the back of her neck. "More."

Her mouth latches onto my clit and my legs begin trembling as ripples of pleasure rip through me like a tornado in an empty field.

My orgasm is so intense, I almost forget there's some freak watching us.

Until he comes into focus and I realize he isn't just some random freak after all.

He's Stone DaSilva.

My arch enemy.

Motherfucker. This just went from bad to worse.

"Go home," I tell Morgan as I slide off the hood of her car. "Now."

Her mouth drops open. "Seriously—"

"Yes," I hiss.

I need her to leave so I can take care of Stone on my own. I don't want her to know he was recording us because she'll just freak out and make everything worse and then he'll never give up the goods.

I just have to reason with him.

And if that doesn't work...well, I'm not opposed to using other tactics to get what I want.

Morgan's expression is full of hurt as she drives off...at the same time Stone starts running away.

Not so fast, asshole.

Sucking in a breath, I chase after him.

Given I'm in such good shape, I'm on his heels in seconds.

"Fucking hell," he exclaims as I land on top of him.

"Give me the phone. *Now.*"

He has the nerve to laugh. "Not a chance."

We wrestle on the dock for the better part of a minute.

Unfortunately, it ends with him on top of me, pinning me to the ground. "You're a real piece of work, you know that?"

I narrow my gaze. "Did you enjoy the show?"

The bulge pressing against me tells me he did. *Gross.*

His expression hardens. "You mean the one where you manipulated that poor girl into—"

"Morgan didn't do anything to me she didn't want to do."

Unless he's blind, it's obvious everything that happened between us was consensual.

Grunting, he stands up. "I heard everything, Bianca. You implied you wouldn't give her a spot on the team unless she *pleasured* you." He jabs a finger in my face. "There's a word for that, you know."

As if. "You must have missed the part where she was very clearly enjoying herself." I drop my eyes to his crotch. "And by the looks of things, she wasn't the only one."

I swear I hear his teeth clack. "That's not the point."

Hands on my hips, I glare at him. "Then pray tell, what is the point of your little moral temper tantrum, DaSilva?"

He groans. "I am so tired of all you fucking Covingtons thinking you own the world and can do whatever you want to people." Face twisting, he gestures to his phone. "I can't wait to give you a dose of your own medicine."

Yeah, that won't be happening.

"You do realize if you show people that you'll be ruining Morgan's life, too, right?"

He shrugs like it's no big deal. "I'll blur her face out." His teeth flash white. "Can't say the same for you though."

Well, shit. He's clearly put some thought into this.

Not a problem. Everyone has a price.

Even moral assholes like Stone.

"How much do you want?"

He looks at me like I'm crazy. "Do you honestly think you can buy me off?"

Duh.

"You're poor as shit," I remind him. "Of course I can buy you off." Pulling out my own phone, I log into my PayPal account. "Just tell me how much it will take to make this little problem go away so we can both move on with our lives."

He laughs, but there's no humor. "Wow."

"Wow, *what?*"

He brushes past me. "Don't worry, princess. I'm sure all the creeps on Pornhub will love watching you come just as much as I did."

He's almost at the end of the dock when I call out, "So you *did* enjoy it."

I knew it.

Flipping me the bird, he keeps walking.

Thinking quick, I sprint over to his car before he gets inside. "Look, there has to be *something* you want."

His stare is downright venomous. "I don't want a damn thing from you."

That's not possible.

Bile surges up my throat as it becomes clear to me what I'm going to have to do to get his phone.

I have no choice, though because I'm not going to let him put that video on a porn site.

Taking his hand, I place it on my tit. "Everyone wants *something*, Stone."

Including nosy, broke losers like him.

He yanks his hand back like he's been burned. "Not interested."

The tenting in his jeans tells me that's bullshit.

"You sure about that?" Trailing a finger up his stomach, I lean in. "You sure you don't want to force me on my knees?" I lick the shell of his ear. "Make the wicked princess suck you off."

When I was fourteen, I paid Bradly Benson one-hundred dollars to teach me how to give a good blowjob.

He'd recently come out as gay, so I figured he was the best person to ask.

And he was.

He was also the best person to practice my *lessons* on.

Therefore, I'm capable of doing things to Stone that will make his head spin and his toes curl.

Poor, sweet Stone looks like he's fighting an internal battle with himself.

It would almost be comical if it wasn't so serious.

"Come on, Stone." I palm his growing cock through his jeans. "Stop being a good boy and teach me a lesson."

I'm fully expecting him to turn me down, but to my surprise he grunts, "Get on your knees."

That's two for two tonight.

Only this one is way worse.

Because it's Stone DaSilva.

The younger brother of the most vile piece of shit on the planet.

Humiliation colors my cheeks as I sink down to my knees and he lowers his zipper.

This was a terrible idea.

But it's too late, because I've already agreed and *he's* pulling out his dick.

To Stone's credit, it's marginally bigger than the fake baby cock I photoshopped onto pictures of him back when he attended Royal Hearts Academy.

I open my mouth, then pause.

My second thoughts about doing this are enough to make my insides churn.

Stone must sense this because he says, "Forget it. I don't want you doing something you don't—"

I take him into my mouth as far as I can.

I need that video.

He punches the side of the car with his fist as I gag myself on his cock. "Fuck."

In for a penny, in for a pound.

That said, I can't deny the sick sense of pleasure I feel at having him at my mercy like this.

I might be the one on my knees, but it's obvious he's not the one in control.

I am.

His face strains as I deep throat him again, trying my hardest to figure out where he put his phone since he's no longer holding it.

He groans. "Jesus fucking Christ, Bianca."

I know.

Placing both of his hands on the back of my head, I start feeling around his pockets.

Low, gruff noises tear out of him as he fucks my face. "Shit."

My heart beats faster. Every inch of him is hard and tight with arousal, ready to explode at any moment.

Focus, Bianca.

Disappointment hits like a brick to the head as I search his first pocket and come up empty.

I take him deeper, sucking him hard and fast as I dig my fingers into his ass.

Jackpot.

I snatch his phone out of his back pocket at the same time a thick stream of liquid fills my mouth.

Standing up, I wipe the corner of my mouth.

Then I spit his cum in his face. "Wow. That didn't take long at *all*."

Anger mixed with disgust tightens his features as he lifts his shirt and wipes off his face.

I take the opportunity to hightail it to the docks, running as fast as I can.

The second I'm near the water, I throw his phone.

I hear his footsteps behind me, but it's already sinking to the bottom.

Mission accomplished.

"You're too late," I inform him.

"And you're seventeen," he sneers.

I have no idea what my age has to do with anything.

I spin around to face him. "What's your point?"

"You could have called the police and had me arrested. Or called your brothers and had them take care of me." He takes a step closer. "But you didn't...you gave me head instead." I hate the cocky smirk on his face. "Which means you wanted to suck my dick, Bianca Covington."

Jesus. The *audacity*.

"No, I did—"

I don't get a chance to finish my sentence because he pushes me into the water.

Chapter 17

"*M*organ," I all but squeak as she starts unbuttoning my shirt.

It's clear the old me had no problem using her, but this Bianca?

She's not really feeling this.

She also doesn't want to hurt her feelings.

"You're amazing," I tell her, gently pushing her away. "But I… everything is just so…" I gesture between us. "I can't do this."

Her face falls. "Oh."

"It's *not* you," I quickly say. "It's me. Ever since the accident, I haven't really been myself."

Ain't that the truth.

"Right," Morgan says. "I didn't mean to…I was just so excited to see you." She picks up my crutches and hands them to me. "How are you?"

That is a loaded question.

"I, uh…I'm having a tough time," I tell her honestly.

"Yeah, I can imagine." She exhales sharply. "I can't believe Hayley's dead."

Guilt prickles my chest because she's been the last person on my mind.

Even though we were friends.

Heck, *more* than friends, if the rumors are true.

"Yeah," I say softly. "I know."

107

Morgan's features twist, like she's contemplating something. "Bianca?"

"Yeah?"

She wrings her hands. "I just don't understand why you were with Hayley that night when I told you what she was doing—"

"*There* you are," Sawyer says. "I've been looking all over for you."

I turn my attention back to Morgan because I have to know. "What do you mean? What was Hayley doing?"

"Bianca," Sawyer snaps, her gaze ping-ponging between us. "Cole and Jace are blowing up my phone wondering where you are. I need to get you back home before they go postal."

No surprise there.

I look at Morgan. "I have to go, but can I give you a call later so we can talk more about this?"

Given she knows what happened the night of the accident, I have a *bunch* of questions for her.

Morgan nods. "Yeah…sure."

After programming her number into my new phone, I hobble out the door. "Ready when you are."

We're halfway out of the restaurant when Sawyer mutters a curse. "I forgot my purse. I'll be right back."

I'm about to offer to go with her, but I spot Stone wiping down the counters.

Suffice it to say, I know *exactly* what happened at the marina now.

As if sensing my stare, he looks up.

Warm eyes move over me like lava, sending a rush of heat through me.

The old Bianca might not have been into Stone…but the new Bianca very much is.

Too bad having feelings for him betrays the people I care about most.

"So, I told Morgan if she wanted a spot on the team, she had to go down on me. What I didn't know was that Stone was lurking and recording the whole thing. I had no choice but to give him a blowjob in order to confiscate his phone and destroy the recording." I hold up my hands. "Well, not *me*. The old Bianca."

The one who ruins *everything*.

Dr. Wilson—or Walter as I usually call him, blinks. "I see."

He promptly jots something down in his notepad.

I blow out a breath. "Anyway, Morgan said something about not understanding why I was with Hayley the night of the crash. I wanted to get clarification, but Sawyer walked in and said my brothers were looking for me." Sighing, I add, "I was supposed to call Morgan later and find out what happened, but she never picked up."

And she's been ignoring me ever since.

A thick, heavy feeling pushes through my chest. "I'm starting to think it might not be such a bad thing, though."

Walter looks up from his notebook. "Why is that?"

I tell him the truth. "Because the old Bianca caused nothing but problems. Maybe it's best I try and move on with my life...well, the one I have now."

Maybe the accident was the universe's way of giving me a second chance.

Chapter 18

a loud thwack zaps me out of my thoughts.

I glance down at the book I dropped. *Awesome.*

I try to bend and maneuver as much as I can to grab it, but I only end up kicking it across the hallway instead.

"Good job, klutz," I mutter to myself.

I hate these stupid crutches.

I look around to see if someone can help me, but there's not a friendly face in sight.

Turning back to my locker, I grab a textbook for a different class.

"I think this belongs to you."

Stone's voice melts over my skin like butter in the midday sun.

Refusing to make eye contact, I drop my gaze to the floor as I take my book from him. "Thanks."

"So, it's like that now, huh?"

It has to be.

Anger fills his voice. "You're not even gonna look at me?"

"You know we can't be friends." Pressing my forehead against my locker, I close my eyes. "Don't make it any harder than it already is."

He leans in just close enough that I can smell his orange-scented soap and the cinnamon from his gum. "You're a fucking coward."

The insult sends my insides coiling.

"Tell me what Tommy did was wrong." Anger flushes over my

cheeks and I find myself glaring. "Look me in the eyes and tell me he's a heartless piece of shit."

That he's responsible for what happened to Liam.

And if there were any justice in the world, it would be Tommy in that grave instead of my brother.

Stone stays silent.

I hobble past him. "Looks like I'm not the only coward."

"*W*ho does that car belong to?" I ask Jace as he pulls into the driveway.

The pink Mercedes convertible has been taking up space in our driveway since I've been here, and I've never seen anyone drive it.

His expression is inscrutable when he answers. "Yours."

"Mine?" I question.

"Yup."

That doesn't make any sense. "I don't drive."

As far as I know, I've never driven.

Your mother dying in a car accident will do that to you.

Jace eyes the car in question. "Dad got it for your eighteenth birthday."

I'm not really sure why he did that, but it's a shame for such a nice, *expensive* car to sit there and rot.

"Well, if you ever want to take it for a spin, feel free." Stepping out of his vehicle, I close his car door. "It's not like I'll be driving it anytime soon."

Or *ever*, for that matter.

Past...

"*J*-j-just s-s-sit in the c-c-car for one m-m-minute," Liam insists as he drags me to our father's car.

Folding my arms across my chest, I stomp my foot. "No."

I'll *never* step foot inside a car again.

Cars kill people.

I narrow my eyes. "Why won't you quit bugging me about this?"

He pouts. "Because I'm t-t-tired of w-w-walking to and from s-s-school every day. I'm t-t-tired of never g-g-going anywhere f-f-fun." He kicks a rock across the driveway. "It's been nine m-m-months."

Nine months, eight days, and four hours.

"You can go places without me," I remind him.

Heck, Jace and Cole do it all the time.

He looks at me like I'm insane. "That's no f-f-fun."

"Neither is being trapped inside something that will kill me."

He grabs me by my shoulders. "I'm your b-b-big b-b-brother."

I have no idea where he's going with this. "Duh. What's your point?"

"I'd never l-l-let anything b-b-bad happen t-t-to you." I fight the urge to remind him that we were both in the crash that killed Mom as he spins me around. "C-c-close your eyes."

Nope. He can't fool me. "I'm not falling for that, Liam."

He huffs. "J-j-just t-t-trust me."

"I swear to God if you push me in that car, I'm punching you in the face."

"I w-w-won't." He loops his pinky with mine. "Pinky s-s-swear."

Dang. Nothing trumped a pinky swear. It was the holy grail of promises.

But still, I didn't want any part of going in that car. "Liam—"

"C-c-close your eyes. P-p-please."

"Fine," I relent. "I'll do it. But if you—"

My sentence falls by the wayside as he places something around my neck.

"What are you doing?"

"O-o-open your eyes."

I finger the thin black lanyard, inspecting the silver pendant dangling from it.

Embedded in the metal is a man trudging through the ocean while holding a staff. Upon closer inspection, I notice he's also carrying a baby on his back.

"What—"

"It's S-s-saint C-C-Christopher," Liam tells me. "He's s-s-supposed to p-p-protect t-t-travelers."

I want to protest and tell him a piece of metal won't save anyone, but he looks so happy. *Like he just discovered the cure to finally fix me.*

I don't have the heart to crush him.

"I can't believe you got this for me."

He shrugs like it was no big deal. "Of c-c-course I d-d-did. I love you."

I blink, unsure how to respond.

Mom used to always tell us she loved us and that it was important to tell each other every day, but ever since she died…

We stopped saying it.

It's as if our love died with her.

With a shaky breath, I reach for the door handle and climb into the back seat. "Fine, I'll do it. But only for *one* minute."

His smile is so bright it could rival the sun.

Chapter 19

"*L*et's go," Jace gripes from the doorway of my bedroom. "You're gonna be late for school."

School can wait.

I frantically continue searching through my jewelry box and every nook and cranny of my dresser but come up empty.

"What are you looking for?"

"Do you remember that St. Christopher pendant Liam got me when we were kids?"

Jace nods. "Yeah."

I look at him. "It's missing."

Along with the silver feather charm I paired with it shortly after his death.

It was my way of acknowledging that he was my guardian angel.

Given I never would have taken it off, it has to be around here somewhere.

Unless…

My heart falls. "Do you think I lost it in the accident?"

I don't have any recollection of it of course, but it's not entirely out of the question to assume it might have fallen off when I went through the windshield.

Jace squeezes my shoulder. "Tell you what, after I drop you off at school, I'll run down to the police station and the hospital and see if it's there."

I wrap my arms around him. "You're the best, you know that?"

I honestly couldn't have gotten through these last couple of months without him and Cole by my side.

I might be broken, but our family is stronger than I ever remember it being.

Mom would be proud.

"I know." He playfully thumps me on the head with the banana in his hand. "Eat this on the way to school."

*L*ike a moth to the flame, my eyes land on Stone.

Unlike the rest of the students in the cafeteria, Stone isn't sitting with a group.

He's a loner who keeps to himself.

Seems we have that in common.

Averting my gaze, I look down at my tray. Today's lunch is pizza, which is preferable to the usual crap they serve. However, it does nothing to lift my spirits.

I miss him.

Even though I shouldn't because he's related to that evil, vile scumbag responsible for Liam's pain.

I'm about to give up on lunch, but Mercedes and her group of bitches surround my space like ants on a popsicle stick.

Here we freaking go.

The irony. Ever since my mom's fatal crash, I've hated the Mercedes brand of cars.

Turns out the humans aren't much better.

"Carmen said she saw you at Cluck You the other day." Before I can remind her it's a free country and inquire what the big deal is, Mercedes slams her hand on the table, causing my tray to rattle. "I'm gonna tell you this one time, puta. Stay the fuck away from my man or you're gonna catch these hands."

I want to ask if she's blind because Stone and I haven't spoken in over a week, but that would only give her the impression that I'm bowing down to her.

Fuck that. I'd rather swallow broken glass.

I expel an irritated breath. "I'm sorry. Last I checked, Stone dumped you and he was single." I give her a sugary sweet smile. "Therefore, he can't possibly be *your* man."

One of her cronies snorts. "Damn, Ma. She got you there."

"Shut up," Mercedes snaps before turning her attention back to me. "We're working shit out."

I hate the sinking feeling in the pit of my stomach. *This is news to me.*

She swivels her head. "And if you know what's good for you, you'll leave him the fuck alone. Don't make me have to tell you again."

I could agree so she walks away, but she caught me on a bad day.

"Wow," I mutter, feigning astonishment.

"Wow *what?*"

"I'm just surprised is all." I shrug innocently. "I really didn't think he'd forgive you for fucking his brother." My grin is all teeth. "*Puta.*"

Before I can blink, she picks up my can of soda, pours it over my head, and crushes the can against my skull. "Bitch."

Gasps and murmurs fill the cafeteria and through my fizzy haze, I see her fingers curl into a fist.

I steel myself, preparing for the impact.

But it never comes.

"Leave her alone," Stone barks, yanking her away.

Mercedes struggles for a bit, but Stone—and his words—are stronger than she is. "I told you we were done."

Her expression screws up. "Only because *she*—"

"Bianca has nothing to do with it. *I* don't want you anymore, Mercedes. You need to get it through your thick skull and stop acting like an obsessed stalker."

"Burn," someone calls out.

Mercedes' embarrassment is tangible, even though she's trying hard not to show it. "Fuck you." Her eyes harden. "And your small dick."

The cafeteria erupts in hoots and howls.

Hurt flashes in Stone's eyes and before I can stop myself, I shout, "No, he doesn't." Using the table for purchase, I stand. "Trust me, I've seen it." I give her a wink. "It must be your loose snatch."

Mercedes lunges for me again, but this time a security guard comes to the rescue and hauls her away.

It's not long before people focus their attention elsewhere.

Stone's eyes fall on me. "Are you okay?"

"I have a headache now, but I'll live."

He whips off his sweatshirt and hands it to me. "Here."

Given I'm covered in sticky soda, I gratefully accept it. "Thanks."

He gives me a curt nod before returning to his table.

Chapter 20

I'm just here to return his sweatshirt.

At least that's what I keep telling myself as I hobble into Cluck You.

When Sawyer mentioned she was going into work to help feed the homeless after Thanksgiving dinner, I asked if she could give me a ride.

It doesn't take long to spot Stone. He's elbows deep in mashed potatoes and gravy. Giving everyone who passes him a hearty portion with a big smile on his handsome face.

Damn him for being kind *and* ridiculously cute.

Damn my heart even more for swooning.

I try to approach him, but Mr. Gonzales stops me in my tracks. "You...*out.*"

Dammit.

"Come on, Mr. G," Stone calls out from his station. "It's Thanksgiving."

When it's clear Mr. Gonzales isn't going to fold, I add, "I was hoping I could help."

Well, not really. But hey, why not? It's pretty crowded and they look like they can use an extra set of hands.

Stone's eyebrows raise in surprise. "Seriously?"

"Absolutely," I state.

His boss might not be too fond of me, but opening his restaurant to feed the homeless and less fortunate Thanksgiving dinner is commendable and it would be awesome to be part of it.

Mr. Gonzales contemplates this for a moment before he says, "Fine. But today *only*. No exceptions." He pulls a hairnet out of his pocket. "Put this on."

I adjust the hairnet on my head and man the gravy station next to Stone. It's a little hard to maneuver due to my crutches, but I manage to make it work and fall into a rhythm serving people.

I can feel Stone's eyes burning into me like hot coals the entire time.

"What?"

His lips twitch. "Nothing."

That's bullshit. The look I give him conveys my thoughts.

He scoops some mashed potatoes into his giant spoon. "I just never thought I'd see *the* Bianca Covington wear a hairnet and feed the homeless."

"Well, I'm happy to be here." After spooning some gravy on a woman's plate and wishing her a Happy Thanksgiving, I decide to come clean. "Although truth be told, it wasn't the official reason I came here today."

His expression turns peculiar. "Oh, yeah?" He serves the next person. "So why are you *officially* here then?"

I cut my gaze to his. "You." Trying to cover up my fumble, I gesture to my purse on the floor. "I mean, your sweatshirt. I wanted to give it back to you."

Placing the spoon down, he inches closer. "That so?"

Oh, boy. I'm thankful for my crutches because my legs are most definitely turning to Jell-O.

"Yeah." I avert my gaze. "I thought you might want it back."

Fortunately, a few people line up at our stations just then and we quickly get to work loading up their plates.

"Bianca?" he says after what feels like an eternity.

"Yeah?"

"He was wrong."

His voice is so low I almost don't hear him.

"What?"

I need to make absolutely certain I understand what he's saying.

His expression is pained as he repeats himself. "He was wrong."

He blows out a breath. "Hell, Bianca. There were *a lot* of people who were at fault that night. Dylan for playing Liam and going to the dance with him. Jace for never coming clean about his feelings for Dylan…but mostly, it was Tommy." Finally, he looks at me. "He never should have bullied him." Sincerity laces his voice. "And for what it's worth, I am really sorry about what happened to your brother. It sounds like he was a great person."

My heart folds in on itself. *He was.*

I'm so stunned by Stone's heartfelt admission; I almost drop my ladle.

Even though what he said was the truth, I know how hard it must have been for him to acknowledge it.

"Thank you," I whisper, my voice shaky with emotion. "I…uh. That means a lot."

It also makes these feelings I have for him stronger.

He turns back to his mashed potatoes. "And just so we're clear I didn't just say it to make you talk to me again. I really meant—"

"Do you want to hang out tonight?" I blurt out.

I can't help wanting to be around him.

Especially now that I know he stands on the right side of things.

His grin is devious. "Well, I'll be damned. Are you asking me out on a date, Bianca Covington?"

"Maybe." I give him a coy smile of my own. "It depends."

He cocks an eyebrow. "On?"

"Whether or not you say yes."

Please say yes.

He shrugs a shoulder. "Sorry, can't tonight."

Well, that backfired.

Swallowing down a lump of disappointment, I utter. "Oh." I look down at the pan of gravy. "I under—"

"I already have plans to watch *Bourne Identity* with this girl I'm crazy about after work."

I couldn't wipe the smile off my face if I tried.

There's only one problem with our impending plans.

I shoot my gaze to Sawyer, who's happily humming Christmas songs and carving up slices of turkey.

Something tells me she's also the kind of girl who likes to leave her Christmas lights up till February.

"I'll be right back," I tell Stone before I hobble over to where she is.

"I need a favor."

She looks up. "Don't worry. I've got everything under control. Alfonso—the chef—is making more gravy and—"

"I don't need more gravy. I need you to cover for me while I hang out with Stone tonight."

Her eyes become saucers. "Say what now?"

"He admitted Tommy was wrong."

She stops carving the turkey. "Okay—"

"Stone's a good guy, Sawyer. You even said so yourself. And I know it doesn't make any sense but I really, really, *really* like him."

"Really?"

I stifle a groan. "Sawyer."

She wipes her hands on a towel. "I don't know. I hate lying. Especially to Cole. After my heart attack, I promised him I'd never lie—"

"Please," I beg. "Besides, it's not like this is a bad lie. I'm just going to Stone's apartment to watch a movie. I'll be gone three hours *tops*."

She wrings her hands. "I *really* don't want to lie, Bianca."

"I know, but you know how overprotective Jace and Cole are. They'll lose their minds if they find out I'm hanging out with Stone, which really isn't fair because he's a good guy. Plus, I thought we were friends?"

If that doesn't convince her to help me out, I don't know what will.

"We *are* friends." She wafts the air with her hands, like she's trying to take in more air. "Fine. I will cover for you. I'll just tell your brothers you..." Her brows crash together. "Wait a minute. It's Thanksgiving night. Nothing is open."

Crap.

Thinking fast, I utter, "What about the library? You can tell them I'm studying."

She blinks. "I'm pretty sure it's closed."

"Yeah, but would *Cole* know that?"

Cole is far from dumb, but it's no secret that—unlike his fiancée —he prefers sports to academics.

She thinks about this for a moment. "Probably not." She shakes her head. "But Jace might."

Freaking Jace. The boy is a sleuth.

I think about this for a bit and decide the best thing to do is stay as close to the truth as possible.

"Tell them I'm hanging out with a guy from school." I give her a wry smile. "Technically it's not a lie…just a little omission."

She gives me a pointed look. "Yeah, I'm pretty sure telling either of them that you're hanging out with some random guy from school will go over like a fart in church."

She has a point.

"Tell them it's a *girl*." I snap my fingers when it comes to me. "Her name is Mercedes."

Turns out the brat is useful after all.

"Fine." She casts her gaze at Stone who's listening in on our conversation with expressed interest. "But there's no way you can have Stone drop you off later because if they see him, they'll lose their shit." She rubs her temples. "I'll pick you up at his apartment and bring you home." She points two fingers at her eyes and then at Stone. "You've got three hours, DaSilva. Don't make me regret it."

Stone places his hand over his heart. "I'll be the perfect gentleman. You have my word."

Leaning my crutches against the wall, I throw my arms around her. "You're the best. I'm so happy we're gonna be sisters."

"Me too." She worries her bottom lip between her teeth. "And as your future big sister, I'm going to give you some serious advice."

"What's that?"

"You need to tell your brothers about Stone. Sooner rather than later."

"I will."

Eventually.

Chapter 21

"I get why you called me Jason Bourne now," I tell Stone. "It's *exactly* like that."

We're currently sprawled out on the futon in his bedroom watching the credits roll.

Dark eyes assess me. I'm not sure what he sees, but it has his expression turning sad. "Damn. It must be really hard." He inhales deeply. "It would drive me crazy not knowing things that happened or what shaped me into the person I am today."

He's not exactly wrong.

Only everything I find out about the former me makes me dislike myself.

"Yeah, but..." I stop talking because I don't have the courage to say it. Plus, I'm scared he won't understand. "Never mind."

He tips my chin, forcing me to look at him. "What?"

"The more I find out about myself...the harder it is." I swallow against the lump forming in my throat. "Not only because of losing my mom and Liam, but I wasn't a very good person before." I meet his gaze head-on. "And I hate getting flashbacks of who I used to be, because I like the Bianca I am *now*."

A small smile unfurls as he leans his forehead against mine. "I like her too."

Feeling bold, I whisper, "Do you like her enough to kiss her again?"

His answer comes in the form of a slow, sweet kiss that sends tingles across my skin.

I open my mouth, silently pleading for more, but he doesn't give it to me.

He continues kissing me like I'm the most delicate, fragile thing he's ever held in his arms.

It's how I know he won't hurt me.

That I'm safe with him.

I moan when finally—*finally*—his tongue enters my mouth.

I'm so into what's happening between us, I barely hear the knock on the door.

"Stone, I'm home," a woman's voice calls out.

I pull away. "Who is that?"

"My roommate."

He never mentioned anything about having a roommate before. Let alone a *female* roommate.

My jealousy must be evident because he laughs and says, "You should see your face right now." Leaning in, he adds, "Don't worry. She's also the woman who birthed and raised me."

"Crap." I bolt upright because making out with her son on his bed in the dark isn't the first impression I want his mother to have of me.

"Relax. My mom's cool." Getting off the bed, he heads for the door. "I'm gonna go say hi. You can come meet her if you want."

A surge of nerves hit me. "I'm good right here."

"Suit yourself."

The moment he leaves, I regret my decision.

If I want to get to know Stone more, a good place to start would be introducing myself to his family members.

Well, the family members of his I can stomach.

Pulling myself together, I hobble out of his bedroom and make my way to the kitchen.

Where I find Stone helping his mom put away groceries.

Be still my beating heart.

"Hi," I say nervously.

Startled, the tiny woman turns around. She's all of five feet tall with pin-straight, sleek dark hair, and beautiful dark eyes. Her skin is flawless, and her features are delicate.

I can see where Stone gets his good looks from because she's absolutely beautiful.

She's also very quiet.

Blinking, she looks at Stone.

"This is Bianca," he explains. "She's the girl I've been telling you about."

The fact that he talks to his mom about me is…*whoa*.

His mother's gaze flicks my way briefly before returning to her groceries.

Somehow, I feel like she chewed me up and spit me out in a single dismissive glance.

What the *hell* did Stone tell her?

Wanting her to like me, I try again. "Is there anything you need help with? Anything I can do?"

She shakes her head. "No thank you."

So much for that.

Stone walks over and squeezes my shoulder. "Relax."

That's easy for *him* to say. His mother already likes him.

I'm contemplating what to do next when my phone vibrates with an incoming text.

Sawyer: I'm outside.

I peer up at Stone. "Sawyer's here."

He looks about as disappointed as I feel. "I'll walk you out."

I give his mom a smile. "It was nice to meet you."

She says nothing.

Awesome.

"I'm pretty sure your mom hates me," I tell him as we walk down the stairs.

He doesn't seem too concerned about it.

"She's my mom," he says as we reach the bottom. "Therefore, she automatically hates any female her son brings home."

Well, *that's* reassuring. "Great."

I'm about to walk out to the parking lot, but he halts me. "If you stick around, I know she'll like you as much as I do." His face screws up. "Well, maybe not as much as I do because that would be weird."

A laugh escapes me until I replay what he said. "If I stick around? What's that supposed to mean?"

Digging his hands in his pockets, he looks away. "You know exactly what it means, Bianca."

"No, I don't."

I'm gonna need him to clarify before I start thinking the worst.

He expels a heavy sigh. "I'm not like other guys. I have no interest in hitting it and quitting it or wasting my time on some chick who doesn't deserve it."

It's hard not to be offended. "Do you think you're wasting your time with me?"

"I don't know." The intensity in his eyes kicks up a notch. "You tell me."

I give him the truth. "I like you Stone, but this conversation is confusing. What exactly is it that you want from me?"

I'm not sure how the old Bianca was with boys and relationships, but *this* Bianca definitely sucks at it.

"I don't want to play games." He inches closer. "If we're gonna do this, then I want all of you."

How can I possibly give someone all of me when *I* don't even have all of me?

As if sensing my internal struggle, he says, "Forget it. It's obvious you don't want the same thing."

"I do want you, Stone," I whisper. "I'm just really bad at this stuff, you know?"

Reaching over, he strokes my cheek with his thumb, "Well, fortunately for you, I'm *really* good at it." In one fell swoop, he pulls me into his arms. "I just need you to trust me."

"I do trust you."

I have no reason not to.

He tips my chin. "Then tell me you're mine."

My mind says we're moving too fast, but my heart wants everything he's offering.

"I'm yours," I utter.

The edges of his lips curl. "Damn right you are."

He closes the distance between us, sealing the confirmation with a kiss.

Chapter 22

I glare at Dylan from across the dinner table. "Pass the peas."

I'm not sure if she notices the tension in my voice, but Jace definitely does.

"Everything okay?"

"Everything is *fine*," I grit through my teeth as Dylan hands me the bowl.

Everything is not fine.

My mind keeps going back to what Stone said last week about Dylan going to the dance with Liam.

She led him on.

She had to know how Liam felt about her, and still, she went to the dance with him.

And even if it wasn't her intention to hurt him, there's no getting around the fact that she definitely went with Liam to hurt Jace.

Either way you slice it...she was out to hurt one—or both—of my brothers.

It's something that will never sit well with me. *Ever.*

Wiping his mouth with his napkin, Dad looks around the table. He's been eating dinner a lot with us lately. It's kind of nice having him around.

"How are you enjoying your new school?"

"I like it."

Especially now that Stone and I are together.

Cole shoves a forkful of meatloaf into his mouth. "Sawyer said you made a new friend."

I aim my glare toward her. She promised she'd keep me and Stone's relationship a secret a little while longer.

"Mercedes," Sawyer says tightly, nudging me under the table.

Damn. I really need to get better at this whole lying thing. "Oh, right."

Jace takes a sip of his drink. "Well, I'm glad you're making some friends."

"You should bring her by some time," Dylan chimes in. "I'd love to meet her."

I can't tell if she's on to me or not, but I don't like it.

And I definitely don't like her. *Not anymore.*

I stab my meatloaf with my fork. "Yeah, and hey, you know what else might be fun? If you went to the upcoming school dance with her and then made out with her brother behind her back."

Dad starts choking on his food.

Sawyer spits out her drink.

And Dylan turns white as a sheet.

"What the hell is your problem?" Jace barks.

I stand up so fast I almost knock my chair over. "*Her.* She deliberately used Liam and we're all just sitting here like one big, happy family acting like she's not partially responsible for what happened to him."

I'm not sure where all this anger is coming from, but I'm shaking with the force of it.

Dylan drops her napkin on to her plate. "I think I'm gonna head upstairs for the night."

I wish she'd leave permanently.

"I'll go with," Sawyer quickly offers.

My thumb hits my chest. "I'm leaving too."

I start to walk away, but Dad and Cole stand up.

"Don't," I tell them. "I want to be by myself."

With that, I slam the patio door closed behind me and head into the backyard.

I know Jace loves her, but I hate that he doesn't see the part she played in all this.

It's like he's blinded by love.

With an audible groan, I yank my cell phone out of my pocket and shoot Stone a text because he's the only person who will understand my outrage over Dylan.

Bianca: Hey.
Stone: Can't talk right now, Bourne. Busy at work.

Well, that ends *that*.

Stuffing my phone in my back pocket, I wander over to the large in-ground pool.

I've been dying to go swimming, but I'm not allowed to until my doctor clears me for it.

The pretty pink sunset bounces off the reflection of the water and I can't help but admire how beautiful it is.

Too bad Liam isn't here to see it.

Even though there's a mountain of grief in my heart, the main emotion gripping me right now is confusion.

Why didn't he talk to me that night?

Why didn't he tell me what happened?

We told each *other everything*.

Why—on the night he needed me the most—didn't he reach out?

I start crying so hard the pool becomes nothing but a blur.

Not wanting anyone to hear or see me fall apart, I hobble over the cobblestones, heading toward the guesthouse.

Despite the empty space and bare walls, a sense of calm washes over me the minute I close the door.

I have no memories of this place. No emotional ties I can think of.

Yet, for some inexplicable reason, it feels like these walls harbor all my secrets.

All my pain.

I'm not quite sure what the reason behind my fresh set of tears are now.

All I know is it hurts like hell.

It's as if there's a physical hole in my chest that can never be filled.

A vital piece of me missing.

A wave of exhaustion sweeps over me and I stagger over to the only piece of furniture in the entire place.

The mattress in the bedroom.

And then I sob until there are no more tears left to cry.

Chapter 23

*W*ith shaky fingers, I type Hayley's name into the search engine.

Instantly, my laptop spits out a slew of results.

Her birthdate and email. An article from our local newspaper that lists all the people from her graduating class. There's even a picture of her from back when she was on the cheerleading squad at Royal Hearts Academy, a link to her Instagram page, and her obituary.

However, there's absolutely nothing in the search results about our accident.

Not even a local news station covered it.

Hmm. I'm about to try a different search, when there's a knock on my door.

"Come in," I tell Sawyer.

"You have to tell them soon," Sawyer hisses, quickly closing my bedroom door behind her. "Keeping this secret from Cole is killing me."

I close my laptop. "I will. I just want to…" Catching myself, I shake my head. "You wouldn't understand."

Her brown eyes soften. "Try me."

"I want to keep him a little longer."

Stone's been the light at the end of a very long, very dark tunnel and being forced to say goodbye to him is going to hurt so much.

I want more time.

"Okay, you're right." Her features screw up. "I don't understand."

I stifle the urge to say I told her so and tell her the truth instead.

"My brothers are everything to me. Which means I'll never put anyone before them. *Ever.*"

"Still not understanding."

"They're never gonna be okay with me dating him, Sawyer."

And because they're my family and I love them…I'll do what they want and stay away.

No matter how much it might hurt me.

A deep frown works over her face. "Honey…no."

Now *I'm* the one who doesn't understand.

"Yes, it's going to suck at first. Your brothers will flip out and do their overprotective brotherly thing and order you to stay away from him." Walking over to me, she cups my face in her hands. "But, Bianca. Your brothers love you. And I know that above everything else—including any pride or anger they might feel—they want their baby sister to be happy. We *all* do."

I guess I never thought about it like that before. "You really think so?"

She smiles. "I *know* so."

"*J*'m telling Jace and Cole soon," I inform Stone.

We're currently lying on his bed, watching another film in the Jason Bourne series.

Turns out Stone is a *really* big movie buff.

He turns on his side, facing me. "Oh, yeah?"

"Yeah." I run my finger down his stomach. "After Christmas."

His forehead creases. "Why not sooner?"

"I don't want to ruin the holidays."

I figure it's the least I can do before I drop the bomb of all bombs.

"Wow." His jaw tics. "Didn't realize being with me was ruining your life."

That's not how I meant it at all. "Stone—"

"Whatever." He sulks. "I get it, I just hate that we have to sneak around all the time."

"It's only for two more weeks." I kiss the tip of his nose. "After that you'll no longer be my dirty secret."

His eyes gleam with wicked intent. "Dirty secret, huh?"

The energy in the room shifts, causing the muscles in my thighs to clench.

Stone has been the epitome of a gentleman, never pressuring me for anything more than a kiss. But the look he gives me tells me he's ready for more.

So am I.

He palms my breast, squeezing gently. "Is this okay?"

More than okay. "Definitely."

Closing the distance between us, he kisses me.

Goosebumps break out along my flesh as his hand dips lower, skimming the bare skin above the waistband of my jeans.

He pulls back. "Am I hurting you?"

My pelvis is the least of my worries. Besides, it's almost healed.

I shake my head. "Not at all."

In fact, I wouldn't mind if his touch was a little rougher.

The sound of him lowering my zipper is so loud it almost echoes.

My breath hitches when he licks two fingers and slips his hand inside my panties.

Smirking, he brushes the pad of his thumb along my clit. "You like this?"

Biting my lip, I nod.

He repeats the movement, sending tiny little tingles to the sensitive bud.

"You want more?"

Hell yes. "Yes."

His movements are so slow, so gentle.

"Stone."

I need *more.* Deeper, faster, harder.

But he doesn't.

Stone continues building me up, deliberately drawing out every inch of my pleasure.

Ever so slightly, he speeds up his movements bit by bit, bringing me to the brink.

He studies my face as he works me. "You gonna come for me?"

Past...

"*Y*esterday s-s-she w-w-wore a yellow dress." Liam looks over at me. "She looked s-s-so p-p-pretty it gave me butterflies."

It takes everything in me not to roll my eyes. His crush on Dylan is becoming all-consuming.

Brows knitting together, he folds an arm under his head. "And t-t-that's w-w-when I realized."

Turning over, I humor him. "Realized what?"

The tear streaming down his cheek pierces my heart. "That I'll n-n-never be good e-e-enough f-f-for her."

"Liam, that's not true."

If I could have any superpower in the whole wide world, it would be for my brother to see himself the way I see him.

Because if he did, he'd realize how incredible he is.

When other kids are mean—Liam's nice.

When other kids are stupid—Liam's smart.

And when other kids are following their mean, stupid friends because they're too scared to be themselves—Liam always follows his heart.

He's the most courageous person I've ever met.

The world is so much better and brighter with him in it.

Another tear falls. "Yes i-i-it is." He swats his tears with his sleeve. "I'm a f-f-freak."

"You are *not* a freak."

"Everyone at s-s-school s-s-says s-s-so," he argues. "Whenever T-t-tommy m-m-m-makes f-f-fun of m-m-me, everyone laughs. No one ever s-s-stops him." More tears fall. So many they soak the pillow. "Because I'm a l-l-loser."

His words punch straight through my heart. Tommy is a dumb jerk who needs to be beat up.

"Liam—"

"I get now why M-m-mom k-k-killed herself." The agony in his eyes makes me want to keel over. "W-w-we d-d-didn't love her e-e-enough."

Pain slices through my chest.

I did love our mom.

So much I fight the anger I have for her daily.

So much that every day that passes I wish I could have done something—*anything*—to save her.

So much I wish it was me who died instead of her, because maybe, just maybe, Liam wouldn't be so upset all the time and I wouldn't have to keep pressuring him to keep the real reason she died a secret.

"I'm n-n-never gonna have a girlfriend," Liam continues, his sobs growing with each word. "I'm n-n-never gonna get m-m-married." He's so distraught, he begins shaking. "No girl is e-e-ever gonna k-k-kiss me. Because n-n-no one's e-e-ever gonna l-l-love me—"

I press my lips to his.

Not because he gives me butterflies like Dylan gives him, but because I want him to know that no matter what happens, I will always love him, and he will always be good enough.

Liam deserves to have everything he wants and then some.

He jerks his head away. "Yuck." Disgusted, he wipes his mouth with the back of his hand. "W-w-what is *w-w-wrong* with you?"

I'm not sure.

All I know is he was hurting and feeling like no one was ever going to love him, so I wanted to prove him wrong.

Because even though I don't love him like *that*—I do love him more than anyone else in the whole wide world.

He's my favorite person.

However, the look of repulsion he's giving me tells me I seriously screwed up.

"I was just trying to help. You were sad so I wanted to make you—"

"Gross." He jumps off the bed like it's on fire. "You c-c-can't do s-s-stuff like t-t-that, Bianca. You're my *s-s-sister*."

I'm about to pinky promise that I'll never, *ever* do it again, but I can't because he runs out of my bedroom, slamming the door behind him.

*V*omit races up my throat and I bolt upright, pushing Stone's hand out of the way.

Oh, God.

What did I do? What the *fuck* did I do?

"Are you okay?" Stone questions. "What just happened?"

What happened is I'm *sick*.

Sick, sick, sick.

"I—" I try to speak, but bile fills my mouth.

I was only trying to make Liam feel better, but there's no way I can explain that to Stone.

Or *anyone* for that matter.

Because no one will *ever* understand.

My intentions were good…but my actions were wrong.

So very wrong.

Oh, God. I can't breathe.

It's too much.

The old Bianca—everything she did—is too much for me to take.

She's like slow poison killing me piece by piece, and I want her *gone*.

"Bianca," Stone says slowly. "Did someone hurt you?"

I should deny it and tell him the truth.

But I can't because he won't understand.

No one will.

I quickly button my pants. "I have to go."

He wraps his fingers around my wrist, halting me. "You can tell me anything."

Not this.

"Please stop," I choke out.

"You got it." Kissing my forehead, he wraps his arms around me. "How about we just lay here for a little bit?"

I drop my head to his chest, breathing in his scent.

"You're okay," he whispers. "Everything's okay."

But it's not.

Because I think I finally know the reason Liam didn't come to me the night he killed himself.

And I have no one else to blame but myself.

Chapter 24

"*I* miss him so much," Dylan chokes out. "So damn much."

My ears perk up and I stop in my tracks, eavesdropping on her conversation with Sawyer.

"I know," Sawyer says.

There's a long pause and then...

"Why don't you go see him?"

"I can't." Dylan sighs. "Jace knows my schedule like the back of his hand. There's no way I'd be able to sneak away without him questioning my whereabouts."

A spark of anger lights my belly.

That little tramp.

My brother was the best damn thing to ever happen to her and she's *cheating* on him?

"I can cover for you," Sawyer suggests. "We can tell him we're having girl time at the mall."

My mouth drops open in shock.

Wow. For someone who gave me so much shit about coming clean to my brothers about Stone, Sawyer has a lot of nerve offering to cover for Dylan so she can run off and screw someone else.

"Thanks," Dylan says. "You're a—"

"Two-timing *whore*," I scream, hobbling into the living room. "How the hell could you cheat on Jace!"

Blanching, Dylan springs up from the couch. "Cheat on Jace? What the—"

"What the hell is going on?" Jace questions behind me.

I spin around to face him. "I overheard your girlfriend making plans to see some guy behind your back."

Jace's eyebrows shoot up in surprise. "What?"

Dylan and Sawyer open their mouths to speak, but I don't give them the chance.

"Dylan kept talking about how she missed some dude and then Sawyer offered to cover for her so she could go see him without you suspecting anything."

Sawyer's jaw practically hits the floor. "Wow."

"Wow *nothing*. Helping Dylan cheat on my brother was wrong and you know it."

"I'm not cheating on your brother," Dylan shouts.

"You were making plans to see him?" Jace questions.

He's so visibly irate and hurt a knot forms in my chest.

Anger crosses over Dylan's features and it makes me want to punch her because she has no fucking right to be angry.

"Yes, I was," she hisses. "God, I am so tired of you *never* understanding where I'm coming from. He's my—"

"Dylan," Jace growls. "Not here."

Snorting, she looks at me. "Right."

I take a step in her direction. "You know what? I think you should leave."

She already hurt one brother and I'm not going to stand here and let her hurt another one.

Over my dead fucking body.

She snatches her purse off the coffee table. "That's a *great* idea." She glares at Jace. "I'll be back for the rest of my shit later."

His face falls. "You're leaving?"

Dylan's eyes become glassy. "I always thought we could make it through anything." Her voice drops to a painful whisper. "But I'm not so sure we can make it through this."

With that, she walks out the door.

Breaking my brother's heart in the process.

"Fuck her," I utter. "She doesn't deserve you."

"You don't know what the fuck you're talking about, Bianca," Jace snaps.

Growling, he launches the glass he's holding at the wall, causing it to shatter and Sawyer to jump.

Then he stalks off, nearly running straight into Cole who's walking into the room.

Looking around, Cole takes a big bite of the sandwich in his hand. "What'd I miss?"

Crossing her arms, Sawyer glares daggers at me. "Your little sister causing trouble." I open my mouth to defend myself, but then she says, "I thought you changed for the better, but it's clear you haven't."

"What's *that* supposed to mean?"

"If you would open your eyes and your heart and stop hating her for two seconds, you'd realize just how much Dylan loves Jace and your family," she snaps. "The girl is putting her *own* pain aside to be there for Jace and you, and—" An irritated groan rips from her throat. I don't recall ever seeing her so upset before. "You were wrong, Bianca. So fucking wrong."

I'm about to ask what she's talking about, but she brushes past me.

"Bible Thumper," Cole calls out after her, but she waves him off.

He turns to me. "What the hell did you do?"

I have no idea. However, something tells me I seriously messed up.

Chapter 25

"*T*hanks." I close the car door. "If I'm not out in twenty, you should probably call the police because one of us most likely killed the other."

Cole snorts. "Duly noted."

I rub my sweaty palms on my jeans and grab my crutches from the back seat.

I didn't plan on coming to Jace and Dylan's apartment but when I asked Sawyer where she might be so I could talk to her, she caved and told me she was here.

I might not like Dylan for what she's done in the past, but I'm willing to hear her side of things because Jace is so damn miserable without her it's hard to look at him.

Drawing in a deep breath, I knock on her apartment door.

It opens a moment later.

Dylan's eyes are puffy, like she's been crying all day. "What do you want?"

"Can we talk?"

Her eyes narrow. "That depends, are you gonna call me a whore again?"

I shrug. "Only if you're cheating on my brother."

She steps to the side, gesturing for me to come in. "I'd *never* cheat on Jace."

The sincerity in her eyes tells me it's the truth.

But if that's the case, I don't know what to make of what I over-heard this morning.

I hobble to the couch and take a seat. "Then who was this guy you missed so much and wanted to see behind his back?"

Sighing, she pinches the bridge of her nose. "My father."

Color me confused. "Huh?"

She opens the fridge, takes out two bottles of water, and hands me one.

"My dad's in jail again."

Stone's words from a few weeks ago flit through my head.

I love Jace, but plastering photos of her dad's mugshot all over school was fucked up.

So was me jumping to conclusions.

"I'm sorry."

She plops down on the far side of the couch. "Yeah, me too."

A weird thought occurs to me. "Why would you need to hide seeing your dad from Jace?"

Jace is all about family so it makes no sense to me.

I'm not sure what to make of the expression on her face. "Because he wants me to stay away from him."

"Why?"

"Um…" She swallows hard. "Well…let's just say he made a *really* bad mistake and your brother no longer thinks he's a good person."

"But he's still your dad. Your *family*."

Jace is the most stubborn person I've ever met, but I can't see him *forbidding* Dylan to see her own father.

But if he did, well…I guess I can see why she'd want to sneak around.

"I know," she whispers, sadness flickering in her eyes.

It makes sense now why Sawyer said she's been putting her own pain on the backburner to be there for Jace.

For *me*.

The girl has been dealing with a lot.

"Boy, I really screwed up, huh?"

A small smirk touches her lips. "Kind of." She shrugs, that sadness returning again. "But Jace and I were bound to have it out about this sooner or later."

I know she's only saying that to make me feel better, but it doesn't.

In fact, it only makes me feel worse…about everything.

Wondering how wrong I've been about other things, I can't help but ask, "Why didn't you turn Liam down when he asked you to go to the dance?"

I need to know if she intentionally used him to get back at Jace.

She exhales sharply. "Because I had no idea Liam liked me like that. He told me he wanted to go as friends and that's honestly what I thought we were."

I'm not sure I believe that. "You *had* to know he had a crush on you."

She looks me in the eyes. "I didn't. Liam was always nice and sweet to me, but I never thought it was anything more than Liam being Liam because he was like that with almost everyone." Her eyes close. "Plus, my feelings for Jace were so intense…he's all I could see." She looks down. "He's all I ever wanted to see."

My heart hurts for Liam. *He never stood a chance.*

"Oh."

"Bianca?"

"Yeah?"

"If I could change everything about that night, I would." Her eyes fill with tears. "Most nights I lay awake wishing my dad made us move one night earlier because then *everything* would be different." She wipes her tears with the back of her hand. "I love Jace, more than anything or anyone…but if I had to give him up so he could still have Liam…I would." A choked sob escapes her. "I swear to God, I would."

Now, *I'm* the one who's crying.

I've had it so wrong for so long.

Liam's death wasn't her fault.

It was just a horrible twist of events that ended in a terrible tragedy.

And hearing her profess that she'd give up Jace if it meant we'd have Liam back…

It's not something a bad person would say.

"I can see why Liam loved you." I cut my gaze to her. "And why Jace does."

She sniffles. "Thank you for *finally* hearing me out."

"Dylan?"

"Yeah?"

Nerves flutter in my stomach because there's always a chance she can tell me to go fuck myself and she'd have every right to at this point. "Can we be friends?"

She gives me a small smile. "I'd really like that."

I take a sip of my water. "Well, now that we got that out of the way—"

The sound of the door opening cuts me off mid-sentence.

A second later Jace storms inside like a man on a mission.

Dylan's eyes widen and she stands up. "What are—"

She doesn't get a chance to finish that sentence because Jace kisses her like she's the oxygen he needs to breathe.

Dylan looks downright dizzy when they break apart. "What—"

"I told you I'd burn the world to the ground before I ever lost you again and I fucking meant it."

With that, he kisses her again.

Getting off the couch, I gesture toward the door. "I'm gonna go."

They're both so into their little lovefest, they ignore me.

Good.

Chapter 26

"I heard there's a party at Jordan Romano's house tomorrow night," I inform Stone at lunch. "Maybe we can go."

I know he doesn't like to hang out with kids from our school—or *anyone* for that matter—but I've been attending Royal Manor High for almost a month now and I'd be lying if I said I didn't want to socialize a little.

Making a face, Stone bites into a chicken tender. "Jordan Romano is an asshole." He takes a lengthy sip of his sports drink. "So are his friends."

I can't hide the flicker of disappointment I feel. "Oh."

"Trust me, Bourne, you won't be missing anything. Just a bunch of losers getting drunk and high." Concern mars his features. "Besides, sometimes the parties he throws get out of hand and I really don't want you around that."

I love that he's trying to protect me, but I need to interact with other people besides him and my family.

"All the more reason you should come with me." I bat my eyelashes, hoping he'll cave. "This way you can be my bodyguard."

"I'm *not* going, Bianca." He pushes his lunch tray away. "You shouldn't either."

I get what he's saying but I'm tired of watching movies in his bedroom all the time. "But I—"

Grabbing his backpack, he stands. "I have to go. I'm helping Mr. Reiss in the chemistry lab and he wants me there early."

I look down at my tray of uneaten food. "Right."

He slides two fingers under my chin, tipping my face to look at him. "Don't be mad at me, Bourne. It's only because I care about you." Leaning down, he kisses my lips. "A lot."

I know he does.

👑

I assess my outfit in the mirror.

The black material is silky soft, and the super short length makes my legs look miles long. Also, the strappy heels I paired it with are to die for.

It's still missing something though.

I rummage through my closet. Old Bianca's clothes mostly aren't my style, but even I have to admit she's got some great pieces in here.

Like the deep purple crop jacket.

A smile stretches across my lips as I look in the mirror for a second time. The pop of color was exactly what I needed.

After applying some lip gloss and checking my phone to see where my Uber is, I grab my crutches and head downstairs.

"Where are you running off to?" Jace questions when he spots me.

Shit on a stick.

I chew my bottom lip, pondering what I should tell him.

"Mercedes and I...we're going out to dinner." I lick my lips nervously as I recall the time. "A late-night dinner."

"Oh."

Jace shuffles his feet like he wants to say something, but he's hesitant for some reason.

Finally, he speaks. "Bianca?"

"Yeah."

"We never really talked about it before, and maybe we should have."

He's losing me. "Talked about what?"

He blows out a breath. "I guess what I'm trying to say is, if you and this Mercedes chick are more than friends…I don't want you to feel like you can't bring her around." His eyes cut to mine. "Gay, straight, bi…whatever you identify as. You're my baby sister and I will always love and support you."

Oh, geez.

His words are touching, but they only serve to make me hate myself for lying to him.

Then again, if I came clean and told him the truth about dating Stone, he wouldn't be nearly as supportive.

He'd be downright homicidal.

I smack a kiss on his cheek. "You're an amazing brother, Jace."

"Does that mean you'll finally bring her to the house so I can meet her?"

I swallow hard. "Sure thing."

File that under *never*.

The music is bumping, and people are packed inside Jordan's house like sardines when I arrive.

Almost instantly, I regret coming here alone.

Especially when some drunk guy staggers over to me.

"Hey, baby. What's a little hottie like you doing all by yourself?"

Gross.

"I have a boyfriend," I tell him, hoping he leaves me alone.

He looks around. "Is he here?"

"He's in the other room," I fib before walking away.

"Hey," another guy greets me.

Since he didn't greet me with, *hey baby*, I decide to be nice. "Hey."

He gestures to my crutches. "What happened?"

"Car accident."

Wincing, he takes a sip from his Solo cup. "Damn. That sucks." Leaning in, he whispers, "What do you say we go upstairs so I can kiss it better."

Seriously?

"Hard pass."

"Stuck up bitch," he mutters as I brush past him.

I'm about to go into the kitchen because it's way less crowded, but I spot Mercedes and her friends.

I quickly turn the other way and head out the patio doors.

Where I see a bunch of people sitting at a table…snorting some white powdery substance.

"Want a hit, beautiful?" some guy asks. "It's fucking *fire*."

Yeah, so *not* my scene. "No thanks."

Sighing, I shuffle my way through the crowd of people dancing in the living room and head upstairs to find a bathroom.

Past…

"**G**od, I'm *so* drunk," Hayley slurs as I lead her up the staircase at Christian's house.

"Me too."

Only unlike the alcohol running through her system, I'm drunk on pure *vengeance*.

Tugging a fistful of her long blonde hair, I pull her in for another kiss.

Her tongue greedily brushes against mine, and I can taste the Malibu rum on her breath.

"Wow," she whispers against my mouth. "You're such a good kisser."

Ugh. I definitely can't say the same about her.

Hayley's kisses are as sloppy as she is…and that's saying something.

I twist the knob of the first door we come to and find it empty.

Closing it behind me, I utter, "Get on the bed."

"Wha—"

I kiss her with more urgency as I walk us backward toward the bed. A moment later we're tumbling onto the mattress with me on top of her.

Arching my back, I grind my pelvis against hers as I skim my lips along the column of her throat.

The perfume she wears is as cheap and trashy as she is.

"That feels so good," she breathes.

Sticking to the plan, I cup my hand between her legs. The lace of her panties feels warm and damp against my fingers. "It's about to feel even better."

Hesitation flickers in her eyes. "I've never done this before…you know…with a *girl*."

"Me either." I skim the length of her pussy over the wet lace. "But like they say, there's a first time for everything."

And sometimes innocent people have to pay for the sins of others.

Smiling, she tugs down the top of my dress, exposing my tit.

Her tongue circles my nipple before she suctions her mouth around it. "You have really nice boobs."

Christ. Even her dirty talk is boring as fuck.

Slowly, I slide down her body until I'm kneeling in front of her. "You're so fucking sexy."

About as sexy as a root canal.

She giggles. "Have you seen yourself? You're like…out of this world gorgeous. So *exotic*."

It's all I can do not to roll my eyes.

I press my lips to the inside of her thigh. "You know what would be really hot?"

Drawing herself up on her elbows, she looks down at me. "You eating me out?"

I'd rather fuck my cunt with a cactus.

Hooking my fingers into the sides of her panties, I slide them down her long legs. "If you gave me a little show."

She blinks. "You want me to play with myself?"

Biting my lip, I nod.

She falters. "I've never done that in front of anyone before."

No surprise. The girl is as alluring and exciting as wet toilet paper.

What the fuck did he ever see in her?

Inwardly groaning, I move my head between her legs, kissing her pubic bone. "If you want me to lick this pussy, you have to show me how you like it."

She moans. "Damn. That feels so—"

"Do it." I scrape my teeth along her flesh, hoping she feels the sting. "It will be fun."

Parting her thighs, she circles her entrance with her finger. "Like this?"

"Give me more, sexy. Rub that clit for me."

Head lulling back, she proceeds to do what I ask. "God, I'm *so* drunk right now."

No, she's not. If she was *so* drunk she'd be puking or passed out…not asking me to go down on her.

She just wants a crutch to blame her actions on—in this case, messing around with a *girl*—so she doesn't have to take responsibility.

At least I own my shit.

"Just like that, babe." Smirking, I take my phone out of my purse and press the record button. "Keep going."

Closing her eyes, she bucks her hips, rubbing her clit with more vigor. "Feels so good."

I couldn't hold back my smile if I tried. The idiot is so into what she's doing, she has no fucking idea what *I'm* doing.

"Good girl, Hayley," I mewl as I angle the camera up a little, making sure I get a glimpse of her face. "Now show me what a dirty little slut you are and how hard you can make that pussy come for me."

A few moments later, she orgasms with a furious shudder, moaning my name.

I make a mental note to bleep my name and disguise my voice before uploading it to every porn site I can think of.

"That *was* fun." Her chest rises with deep exhales and beads of sweat trickle down her brow. "You gonna go down on me now?"

Nah, I'm gonna ruin your fucking life, bitch.

Yours and his.

Slipping my cell back into my purse, I stand. "Can't, baby doll. Big bro number two keeps blowing up my phone asking where I am, so I'm pretty sure someone tipped him off about our little make-out sesh downstairs." I blow her a kiss. "Thanks for the show, though. Maybe we can do it again sometime."

Keep your friends close and your enemies closer.

Chapter 27

*W*hat. The. Actual. Fuck.

Two thoughts hit me in rapid succession.

One—Hayley and I were definitely *not* friends because I clearly hated her for some reason. And two—given my severe hatred, why the hell was I in the car with her that night?

Rubbing my temples, I let out a silent scream.

I knew my former self was fucked up, but this is…setting her up like that…

It makes me sick.

Especially since I'll never have the chance to apologize.

I ruined this poor girl's life…and now she no longer has one.

Splashing some cold water on my face, I force myself to breathe.

Once I'm calm enough, I grab my crutches and hobble back down the staircase.

I might not be able to tell her I'm sorry, but it's not too late to go home and do the right thing.

"Someone call the cops!" a girl screams as I walk into the living room.

Nerves bunch in my tummy as I watch two guys in what looks to be a *very* heated altercation.

"I want my money," some guy barks.

"I told you," the other guy says. "I don't have it right now."

The first guy pulls a gun out of his waistband and fires a bullet into the ceiling, causing my ears to ring so bad I automatically cover them with my hands. "Then I guess you give me no choice, motherfucker."

Holy shit. Stone told me these parties got out of hand, but I didn't think he meant *this.*

My eyes flick to the front door. It's about eight feet away from where I'm standing which means I can easily walk out.

"No one move," the guy with the gun sneers. "I'm about to show all of you what happens when you fuck with me."

I'm not sure about everyone else, but I definitely don't need a demonstration. *I'm good.*

My heart is beating so hard I'm afraid it's going to pound right out of my chest.

Stone was right. I *never* should have come here.

"Get on your knees," he instructs, pointing his gun at the other guy.

Oh, God. He's going to shoot him right here in front of everyone.

The sound of the gun cocking echoes throughout the room as he holds it up to his temple.

I can't watch. "Please do——"

"Police," a deep voice booms on the other side of the front door. "Open up."

"Oh shit," someone yells. "Run."

Utter pandemonium breaks out as everyone starts rushing toward the exits.

Except me...the girl with crutches.

Fortunately, most people run out back which means the front door is wide open when the cops come busting through.

Frantically, I fish my phone out of my purse as I hobble past them.

Stone picks up on the second ring.

"Hey——"

"I should have listened to you. There was a guy with a gun and he——"

"Wait, what?" Stone yells. "Where the fuck are you?"

"I went to the party at Jordan's——"

"Are you serious?" he shouts. "I told you not to go."

I want to argue that he said I *shouldn't* go, but now is not the time for semantics.

"Can you come get me? Please."

"On my way."

J spot Stone's red Chevy on the opposite end of the street in record time.

I'm about to walk over, but he steps out of his car, his long strides eating up the ground between us in no time.

His anger is so tangible I can practically taste it. "Are you fucking stupid or something? What part of do *not* fucking go to the party don't you understand?"

Woah. I know he's upset, but this is…excessive.

"I'm not stupid. I—"

Disgust mars his features as he looks me up and down. "What the fuck are you wearing? That dress is so short I can practically see your pussy." His eyes darken when they connect with mine. "You look like a goddamn slut."

My stomach twists at his words and I expel a breath that hurts.

I thought I looked nice.

"You know what? Forget it. I'll find my own ride home."

I pull up the Uber app on my phone because I don't want to be anywhere near him right now.

I start to walk away, but his fingers wrap around my wrist, halting me. "Wait."

"For what? You to tell me I'm stupid again?"

"I was wrong."

The genuine remorse in his eyes tells me he means it, but still.

What he said hurt. *A lot.*

I try to get away again, but my crutches and his iron-clad grip on my wrist make it impossible.

"Look at me, Bourne."

I close my eyes. "I don't want to."

It hurts too much.

He closes what little distance there is between us, cupping my cheekbone. "I'm sorry."

I glare at him. "You called me a slut."

"I'm an asshole. A stupid, jealous asshole." Leaning his forehead against mine, he whispers, "I'm trash…and you're perfect. I feel like I'm constantly waiting for the day when you wake up and realize what a mistake being with me is."

Turns out his little self-fulfilling prophecy just came true. "Well, congrats. That just happened."

I try to walk away again but he tightens his grip. "I fucked up, Bianca. But it will never happen again. I *promise*."

Every fiber in me is telling me to forgive him, but there's a little, nagging voice in my head that can't help but wonder if this is a warning of some sort.

"One more chance," he urges, as if sensing my internal dilemma. "Give me *one* more fucking chance."

I can feel my heart caving. "Stone—"

"Please." He frames my face with his hands. "I don't want to lose you."

I don't want to lose him either.

He's the only good thing to come out of this horrible situation.

Besides, the way he was before isn't like him. At all.

Everyone makes mistakes.

"Tell me I didn't lose you." His eyes are pleading, imploring me not to end what we have. "Tell me we aren't over."

"We aren't over," I whisper.

Because the heart wants what it wants.

Chapter 28

"*H*e used to hit her," Stone whispers.

We're lying in his bed, a tangled mess of arms and limbs wrapped around one another.

My fingers which were stroking his stomach pause. "Who?"

Eyes closing, he inhales deeply. "My dad." Despair mixed with rage colors his voice. "Sometimes he'd beat her so bad my mom would be covered in bruises for weeks…a few times he even broke her arm."

My heart thunders against my chest, hard and painful.

Not only for Stone's mom who had to endure something so brutal and awful, but for Stone who also had to experience it.

It makes even more sense why they're so close.

"I'm so sorry."

He looks down at me. "Tonight scared me because I sounded exactly like him."

My stomach does a strange, sick lurch.

He tips my chin. "But I'm gonna make sure that never happens again." His lips find my forehead. "Because I care about you. So fucking much."

I believe him.

I also can't help but wonder. "You said your dad's in jail, right?"

"Yeah."

The thought of him getting out and hurting Stone's mom again doesn't sit well with me. "When does he get out?"

"Not for another two years." His expression turns stony. "Given all the shit they found in his car when they arrested him, I'm surprised he didn't get more."

"What shit?"

"He was a drug dealer," he spits. "A lowlife fucking drug dealer."

That's definitely news to me. "Oh."

His fingers clench into a fist. "I hate drug dealers…almost as much as I hate him." He cuts his gaze to mine. "The day after he got arrested, I told my mom I wanted to become a doctor. This way I could always take care of her and my family the *right* way."

And that's just one of the many reasons I gravitate to him like a moth to a flame.

Stone could have taken the same path his father did, but he didn't.

He's one of the good ones.

Reaching up, I run my hand along his jaw. "For what it's worth, I'm proud of you for not following in his footsteps."

He presses his lips to mine. "That means a lot."

Skimming my nose along his neck, I breathe him in. "*You* mean a lot to me."

He kisses me again, slow and deep.

Tingles zip up my spine as he slides his palm up my thigh. "You have no idea what you do to me."

A low groan escapes him when his hand dips inside my panties.

"You're so wet," he murmurs against my mouth.

"More," I utter, bucking my hips.

He plunges two fingers inside me.

"Jesus, you're so tight," he groans, working them faster.

My eyes flutter closed against the pressure. It feels so good.

So fucking good.

"Oh, G—" An image of Hayley infiltrates my mind and I bolt up. "Hayley."

I need to find a way to get rid of that video.

Stone is understandably confused. "What—"

"Do you have a computer I can use?"

He gestures to the small laptop on his desk in the far corner of the room. "Yeah, sure. But why do you need one right *now?*"

Forgoing my crutches, I take a seat at his desk and flip open his laptop. "What's your favorite porn site?"

Given he's an eighteen-year-old guy, he's the perfect person to ask.

He looks even more confused as he motions to his raging hard-on. "Trust me, what we were doing got my cock rock hard. You're hotter than any porn out there."

I'd laugh if it wasn't such a dire situation. "That's not why I was asking." I look down at the floor. "I had another flashback at the party."

"What happened?"

I don't want to tell him because I don't want him to judge me, but I need someone to confide in.

"It was bad," I warn him. "*Really* bad."

His expression turns serious. "Bianca, whatever it is, you can tell me."

Taking a deep breath, I lay it all out there. "As usual, I only have bits and pieces to go on, but from what I gather, Hayley and I were making out at some party and I led her upstairs to hook up."

Safe to say I have Stone's undivided attention.

"Okay, so you hooked up with a girl…again. No big deal."

"Hooking up with a girl *isn't* the problem," I interject. "Me intentionally seducing and then tricking her is." I close my eyes because I can't bear to look at him while I tell him the next part. "I made her masturbate in front of me, and while her eyes were closed and she was…you know, *into* it, I recorded her." I swallow hard. "And then I uploaded the video to a bunch of porn sites."

Standing, Stone runs a hand over his scalp. "Damn. That's…"

My insides coil with shame. "Completely fucked up."

"Yeah…yeah, it is." He scrubs a hand down his face. "But that was the old Bianca." His gaze collides with mine. "It's not who you are anymore."

He's right…but still.

"I know." I turn my attention back to his laptop. "But I need to find all the porn sites where I uploaded the video and delete them."

It's the right thing to do.

"Okay, well, the biggest porn site is Pornhub."

I quickly type the name into the search engine, ignoring all the boobs and vaginas that pop up on the screen. "There's a login." I look at him. "I'm guessing that's how one would upload a video?"

Stone blinks. "I mean, *I* have no experience uploading videos. I just watch them—never mind, that's not important." He shrugs. "Login and see what happens."

I start to type in my email then pause, my mind going blank. "I have a problem."

"What?"

"I can't remember my password."

Luckily Jace was able to reset all my passwords for my email and social media sites back when he fixed my laptop, but I'm guessing old Bianca wasn't stupid enough to use her regular email for this.

It would be too easy to track back to her...*us.*

God, I hate this.

"I don't know what to do." My shoulders slump in defeat. "There's no way I can fix this if I don't know what email I used and what my password would be." I snap my fingers when it comes to me. "There's a search engine on the site. Maybe I can just type in her name or something like, young, hot blonde masturbates—"

"Yeah, that's not gonna work." His gaze turns inward. "First, I doubt you used Hayley's actual name in the subject of the video. And two—if you type young, hot blonde masturbates or *any* variation of that into the search engine, you're going to get thousands of hits. It will take you weeks to sort through them all." He huffs out a humorless laugh. "Plus, if you do manage to find it, there's no guarantee the site owners will respond to your email or take the video down." He exhales long and deep. "As much as I hate to say it because I know how much you want to fix this, you're better off letting it go."

I hate this. So fucking much.

"I'm a really shitty person."

"You aren't," Stone argues. "The *old* you was."

Fair enough, but it doesn't make me feel better about what I did.

Or make anything less confusing.

"Speaking of the past, I still don't understand why I was with her that night when I apparently hated he—"

I stop talking because a thumbnail on the bottom of his computer screen snags my attention.

It's a little grainy…but it's definitely me.

My mouth drops open when I click on it and a video of me lying on the hood of Morgan's car with my legs spread open while she goes down on me begins to play.

A million different emotions hit me at once. None of them good.

"What the hell, Stone?"

His eyes widen. "I can explain that."

I spin around to face him. "I threw your phone in the water. How do you still have this?"

I thought I destroyed it.

He looks sheepish. "I emailed the video to myself before you did."

I'm not sure how to feel about this.

Actually, I do.

Despite this being the pot calling the kettle black and karma for what I did to Hayley, I'm pissed.

Old Bianca might deserve this, but *I* don't.

"Why the fuck would you—"

"Because I wanted to keep it."

I glare at him.

"For *myself*," he stresses. "Not to send to anyone else, I swear."

Still doesn't make any sense to me. "Why the—"

"I jerk off to it, all right?" he snaps, the tips of his ears turning pink. "And I get why you're upset, but no one else has ever seen it." He looks me in the eyes. "That's the God's honest truth."

Well that's…*interesting*.

"I thought you hated me…you know, before the accident."

At least that's the impression I got from our first meeting.

The one I can remember.

"I did." Arms crossing over his chest, he plops back down on the bed. "But I also wanted you." His lids lower. "*Badly*."

Oh. "Really?"

His Adam's apple bobs. "Yeah."

I probably shouldn't be so turned on that he kept a video of me he had no right to film, but I can't help myself.

Images of Stone getting himself off to me is…hot.

Really hot.

Reaching for the hem of my dress, I slip it over my head until I'm in nothing but my bra and panties. "Ever think about me stripping for you?"

He licks his lips. "Sometimes."

Slowly, I saunter over to him. "What about my mouth on your cock?"

There's a sharp intake of breath. "Bianca——"

I undo the clasps of my bra and let it fall to the floor. I should probably be embarrassed, but the way Stone's looking at me right now—like I'm the most beautiful girl he's ever seen—fills me with a confidence I didn't know I had.

A low, tortured groan leaves him as he reaches up and squeezes my breast. "God, you're so fucking perfect."

I'm not, but he makes me feel like I am.

Sinking to my knees, I tug down his zipper and pull him out.

He's hard and ready for me.

I give him a slow, teasing jerk. "Tell me what else you think about when it comes to me."

"Just typical fantasies." He visibly swallows. "You and I…you know."

No, I don't. *But I want to.*

Lowering my head, I lick the pearlescent drop of liquid off his crown. "Can you be more specific?"

I want to hear all the dirty, hot words roaming through his mind.

He groans as I lick his length. "What you're doing now…I think about that."

Stretching my mouth over the wide head of his dick, I moan, sending vibrations pulsing through him.

Stone nearly lurches off the bed. "Fuck."

Taking him as deep as I can, I peer up at him.

"Jesus Christ," he rasps as he humps my face. "You're so fucking good." His movements speed up. "So fucking go——"

Salty liquid fills my mouth, and unlike last time, I swallow.

"Shit." Out of breath, he collapses against the bed, but not before I venture into his arms. "I wasn't expecting..." He cups my cheek. "Do you want me to return the favor?"

Shaking my head, I nuzzle against his chest.

I just want him to hold me.

Because the past...all the bad things I've ever done...

None of it matters when I'm with him.

Chapter 29

Sunlight streams through a crack in the curtain, rousing me from my slumber.

Panic shoots up my spine as I take in my surroundings.

"Shit."

I can't believe I fell asleep here.

I quickly nudge Stone who's still sleeping beside me. "Wake up."

Springing off his futon, I search for my clothes.

Yawning, he rubs his sleepy eyes. "What time is it?"

My gaze roams to the clock on the nightstand as I shimmy into my dress from last night. "Just after six a.m."

Which means Sawyer is probably still sleeping and won't be able to pick me up.

A quick glimpse at my phone tells me Jace called three times last night, Cole called once, and Sawyer texted me twice asking if I was spending the night with "Mercedes."

Crap.

Stone pats the empty space beside him. "In that case, come back to bed."

I gape at him. "Are you crazy? I need you to drive me home."

"Now?"

"Yes, *now.*" I grab my crutches that are leaning on the wall beside his bed. "There might still be time to sneak inside without my brothers realizing I never came home."

Then again, Liam and I were always the late sleepers while Jace and Cole preferred to be up at the butt crack of dawn. *Weirdos*.

Jumping to his feet, Stone snatches his keys off the nightstand. "Let's go."

✦

"*I*t seems pretty quiet," Stone notes as we pass my house. "I think it's safe to pull into the driveway."

"Don't," I hiss. "They might see you." I shoot my gaze out the passenger window. "Park down the block."

"You still need crutches to walk, Bianca," he huffs. "I'm not parking down the block."

I open my mouth to remind him that my crutches will be gone in a week, but there's no use arguing.

The quicker I get inside and upstairs to my bedroom, the better.

Given the lights are still off and there's no sign of activity going on in the house, now is the perfect time.

"Fine," I relent. "Park in the driveway. But don't stay and watch me walk inside. The second I'm out of the vehicle you need to flip this bitch in reverse and gun it."

His lips twitch. "Got it, Brian O'Conner."

"Brian O'Conner?"

He looks at me like I'm a space cadet. "*Fast and Furious*."

Still not understanding. "Fast and Furious?"

Sighing, he pulls into my driveway. "We really need to work on your movie—"

"What the actual *fuck* is going on?" Cole roars.

Oh, shit.

I turn my head to face a very sweaty and *very* irate Cole who looks like he just got finished running a marathon.

Not waiting for a response, he brings his cell to his ear. "Jace, get the fuck out here now. Bianca just pulled up with Stone fucking DaSilva."

Goddammit.

I roll down my window. "Relax, Cole. It's not—"

He pounds on the hood. "I swear to God if you hurt her, I will *kill* you."

Oh, for fuck's sake.

Stone looks offended. "I would *never* hurt—"

"What the fuck are you doing with my baby sister, DaSilva?" A shirtless and shoeless Jace booms as he flies down the driveway. "You got a motherfucking death wish, *bitch*?"

It's safe to say the shit has officially hit the fan.

Stone's hand clenches around his steering wheel. "Nope, I don't have a death wish." He must though because he grins. "I was simply dropping my girlfriend off at her house."

"Stone," I snap.

"What?" he says as I step out of his car. "They were going to find out about us soon, Bianca. You said it yourself."

Yeah, but I didn't want them to find out like *this*.

Cole laughs but there's not an ounce of humor. "I've had a few concussions and therefore must be hallucinating, because I could have sworn you just said *girlfriend*." His nostrils flare. "But there's no way in fuck *my* little sister would ever date your pathetic, trifling ass."

He yells the last part so loud he's liable to wake the dead.

A breathless, bathrobe-clad Sawyer runs outside. "What the hell —" She spots Stone's car and blanches. "Oh, shit."

Oh, shit is right.

Jace's jaw tics. "Tell me he's lying, Bianca."

I can't.

Expelling a deep breath, I utter, "He's not."

Cole cups his ear. "I'm sorry, I must be hallucinating again, *what*?"

"He's not lying," I say, louder this time. "Stone and I are dating."

Jace staggers back like I just sucker-punched him.

Cole turns to Sawyer. "Call an ambulance."

She pales. "Are you okay?"

"I'm fine, Bible Thumper." He lunges for Stone's car. "But he won't be after I'm done with him."

Sawyer and I quickly put ourselves between them.

"Feel free to leave anytime," I urge Stone.

"Not until your psycho brothers calm down and I know you're okay."

That only makes Cole more furious and he lunges for him again. "I'll show you psycho."

"Stop it, Colton," Sawyer says, her hands shoving his chest. "Fighting Stone won't solve anything."

"Maybe not," he snarls. "But it will sure feel good."

Before I can stop him, Stone gets out of his car. "You want to fight me again, Covington." He slaps his chest in invitation. "Go right ahead. Kick my ass from here to Kingdom Come." His eyes dart to me. "But it still won't change the fact that I'm in love with your sister."

My mouth drops open. "You *love* me?"

"Yeah." He swallows hard. "Yeah, I do."

Sawyer makes the sign of the cross and starts muttering what sounds like the Hail Mary prayer.

My head whirls. *Stone loves me.*

Cole's eyes flick to me. "Please tell me this isn't fucking happening."

"How long?" Jace barks. "How long have you been lying to my goddamn face while sneaking around with trash?"

"Since Thanksgiving," I whisper.

"A month," Jace bites. "A fucking month you've been deceiving me." He gestures to Cole and Sawyer. "*Us.*"

Sawyer rubs her temples. "Look, I know you two are angry, but Stone's a good guy and he makes her happy—"

"How would *you* know?" Cole questions.

"I—uh." She mutters a curse. "I've known about them for a little while."

The betrayal on Cole's face deepens. "And you didn't tell me?"

"It's not Sawyer's fault," I quickly chime in. "She kept urging me to come clean, but I made her promise not to say anything until I was ready. Hell, she didn't even want to cover for us, but I—"

"You covered for them?" Cole grinds out, glaring at Sawyer. "For *him?*"

Oh, fuck. Wrong thing to say.

Guilt colors Sawyer's rosy cheeks. "I know you're upset, but Bianca's my friend and she needed someone to talk to."

He jabs his chest with his thumb. "*I'm* your fiancé." Hurt twists his features. "Your fiancé who you swore you'd never lie to again."

Sawyer's face falls. She looks so helpless my heart coils.

"I'm sorry, Colton—"

"Save it. I don't even want to be near you right now." His eyes fall on me. "*Either* of you."

With that, he treks up the driveway.

Sawyer's lower lip wobbles. "I—um. I'm gonna go back inside."

Stone juts his chin. "I'm gonna go, too." He leans down like he wants to kiss me but pauses when he notices that Jace is still glaring daggers at him. "I'll call you later."

A minute later he peels out of our driveway.

I look at Jace, who's gone silent.

"Say something."

Yell at me. Demand I break up with him. *Something.*

He shrugs helplessly. "What the hell do you want me to say, Bianca?"

The sheer hurt etched in his features makes me want to keel over and die.

He starts walking away but stops abruptly.

"I really fucking miss her."

I have no idea who he's talking about. "Who?"

"My sister." His eyes cut to mine. "The one who might lie to everyone else in her life but would *never* lie to me."

With that, he stalks off.

I expected him to be angry…disappointed.

But I never expected him to look at me like I stabbed him in the back.

And I definitely never thought I'd break his trust.

Chapter 30

A soul as black as the night sky.
Lips as red as the blood she's out for.
The girl who leaves them running scared.
She's a beautiful nightmare.

I stare in awe at the words scrawled on the small piece of paper.

On one hand, I should be offended because Stone thinks my soul is *black*, but on the other?

It's so hauntingly gorgeous it cuts straight into my heart.

I quickly pick up my phone.

It's been three days since all hell broke loose, but we still talk every day at school. However, I'd be lying if I said I didn't miss our *alone* time.

Especially after reading that.

He picks up on the second ring. "Hey you."

"Hey." I can't help but smile. "So, I was doing laundry today and I found a little something you slipped into my jacket pocket the other night."

"Huh?"

"The poem," I remind him. "Jesus, Stone. I had no freaking idea you wrote poetry. It was perfect. A little dark and twisted…but beautiful."

A beautiful nightmare.

"Oh…that." He clears his throat. "I'm glad you like it."

"Like it?" My heart pounds a steady tattoo against my ribs. "I *love* it."

I rub the spot over the organ still beating wildly in my chest. *I love him.*

But I don't want to tell him something so important over the phone.

I'd rather tell him how I feel face to face. *When the moment is right.*

"So," he says, changing the subject. "Are things any better today?"

Nope. "About the same."

He sighs. "They can't forbid you to see me, you know. You're eighteen."

If only it were that simple. "They're not forbidding me to see you."

That would require they actually *talk* to me.

"So we're not hanging out because you don't want to," he snaps. "Got it—"

"It's not like that," I tell him. "It's just…complicated."

They're my family and I *hate* hurting them.

And as much as I care about Stone, seeing him without their approval feels like I'm committing treachery.

"I know how important they are to you, Bianca. Trust me, I get it. I guess I'm just hoping I'm important to you too."

My heart twists. "You are."

"Then come here for Christmas so I can see my girlfriend outside of school. We're having a late-night dinner after my mom gets off work." He snorts. "I'm in charge of cooking, but I promise I'll try my best to make it edible."

"Okay." I highly doubt everything will be fine in two days, but I really want to see my boyfriend for the holidays. "I'll be there."

I just have to talk to my brothers, first.

J approach Cole first because he's...well, the more approachable of the two.

"Sorry, I don't deal with *traitors*," he greets me after I knock on his door.

I stifle my annoyance. "Can we talk? Please."

Sulking, he gestures for me to come in. "I guess."

I look around his bedroom. Sawyer isn't here, but fortunately, her things still are. "Where Sawyer?"

His sulk deepens. "Work."

There's a slight edge to his tone.

"Cole." I give him a look. "Sawyer didn't lie to you because she wanted to. She lied because I begged her to. Hell, I pretty much guilted her into it."

Pouting, he crosses his arms. "I know."

"Then wh—"

"Because you didn't tell me," he barks. "I know I'm not the best brother and Liam was your favorite and you pretty much consider Jace your dad. I just wish..." His sentence trails off.

"You wish what?"

"I wish you felt comfortable enough to confide in me. Although that's stupid, because it's not like we were tight before your accident —probably because you were still harboring anger for the shitty way I treated Liam when he was alive." He grips the back of his neck. "I don't know. I guess I was hoping since you have amnesia we could press the reset button on our relationship and start over."

His confession makes my heart squeeze. No matter how close I was to Liam or how close I am to Jace, Cole's still my brother.

I give him a hopeful smile. "I see no reason we can't still do that."

He lifts his head a fraction. "Yeah?"

Nodding, I give him a smile. "Yeah."

He raises an eyebrow. "Do we do the awkward hug thing now, or can we skip that?"

I feign disappointment. "Damn. I was kind of looking forward to it."

Opening his arms wide, he sighs dramatically. "All right, fine. Bring it here."

Laughing, I wrap my arms around him. "I might not remember much about our relationship before my accident. But, for what it's worth, you've been a pretty great brother after." I make a face. "A little overprotective—"

"A *little*?" he grunts. "I'm gonna have to up my game then. Call that punk over—"

"Cole," I utter as we break apart. "Please don't beat up my boyfriend."

"Christ." Scoffing, he pinches the bridge of his nose. "I still can't believe you're dating Stone DaSilva."

"He makes me happy," I whisper. "Really happy."

Another scoff. "Yeah, well he better if he knows what's good for him."

My heart does a hopeful little dance. "Does this mean you approve?"

Cole scowls. "Approve? No." Shrugging, he adds, "But fuck knows I've done my fair share of dumb shit, so I guess you're entitled to do some dumb shit, too."

Gee, thanks.

Given that's the best I'm going to get out of him for now, I drop it.

However, there's still one thing I want to fix.

"What about you and Sawyer? You guys aren't going to break up over this, right?"

He looks horrified. "Break up? Fuck no. That's not an option. I'm still mad that she kept it from me, but I know her heart was in the right place. It always is." His gaze turns inward. "It's just one of the many reasons I'm in love with her."

That's a relief.

Shooting him another smile, I close the door to his bedroom.

However, my relief is short-lived when I spot Dylan. "On a scale of one to ten how bad is his mood today?"

"About an eight." She gives my shoulder a squeeze. "I keep reminding him that he's being a stubborn ass though, so I'm sure he'll come around...sooner or later."

Yeah, but *when?* Jace hasn't said a single word to me since the driveway incident.

"Right."

"Just give him time." Her nose crinkles. "Eventually he'll thaw and talk to you."

Unfortunately, I'm running out of time. Christmas is in two days.

Taking my chances, I knock on his bedroom door.

"What?" Jace barks from the other side.

"Can I come in?"

Silence.

"You can't ignore me forever, you know."

Nothing.

Chapter 31

"Stop being a dick to her, Jace," I hear Dylan hiss from the hallway. "It's *Christmas* for fuck's sake and you just made her cry."

"It's not my fault," Jace argues. "All I did was ask if she was lying when she complimented you on the ham you made. Given her *stellar* track record, it was a legitimate question."

I wipe my tears away with a tissue. I'm not sure how much longer he's planning on staying mad at me or making jabs at my expense, but I can't take much more of this.

Dylan growls. "I swear to God, if you don't man up and apologize right now, I'll—"

"You'll *what?*" Jace sneers.

"You know that thing I let you try last week—the thing you *really* liked? Well, it will be a cold day in hell before I ever let you try it again."

Yeah, I definitely don't want to know what *thing* she's referring to.

Jace sighs. "Fine, I'll apologize but it won't change anything. I'm still pissed that she lied."

"Jesus," Dylan exclaims. "Get a grip. With everything she's been through the last thing she needs is for you to turn your back on her because she made a mistake. Plus, you and I both know she only lied because regardless of her amnesia, she still adores the hell out of her big brother and didn't want you to be upset with her."

179

"Whatever," he grumbles.

"Stop being so pigheaded and fix this," Dylan urges. "Because the Jace I know and love would do anything for his family and admits when he fucked up."

A moment later I hear footsteps trek down the stairs followed by a sharp knock on my door.

I hug my pillow to my chest. "What?"

"Can I come in?" Jace questions.

"I guess."

Truth be told, I should ignore him like he ignored me, but unlike him, I know how much it hurts.

I do, however, turn my head and stick my nose in the air when he walks in. *Take that, asshole.*

He makes an irritated noise in his throat. "Seriously?"

I don't warrant him with a response.

His sigh is weary and resigned as he walks around my room, picking up and putting down various objects on my dresser. "I never wanted a sister."

Jesus. That's just *mean.*

I glare at him, and he has the audacity to laugh. "Let me finish."

"Fine. Unlike *you,* I'm willing to listen."

"When Mom told me she was having a girl, I had a full-blown temper tantrum and cried for two days."

"Why?"

"Because I wanted brothers. I didn't want to deal with a sibling I could never identify with." He pins me with a look. "But the day Mom placed you in my arms, this intense sense of obligation came over me and I vowed right there and then that I would always protect you." Scoffing, he shakes his head. "I didn't know it back then, but God is a comedian because my baby sister turned out to be exactly like me—insanely stubborn and guarded, yet fiercely loyal to those she loves." He meets my gaze. "Hell, it probably should have been us who were twins instead of Cole and Liam."

My heart feels like it's going to burst out of my chest.

I hate fighting with him, but even more than that, I hate knowing I broke his trust and destroyed our bond.

"I never meant to hurt you," I whisper. "It kills me that I did."

Hands in his pockets, he nods. "I know."

I peer up at him. "Are you ever going to forgive me?"

He smirks. "Eventually."

I throw my pillow at him. "Stubborn ass."

He throws it back at me. "But just because I'm upset doesn't mean I love you any less."

"I love you too, shithead."

Humor lights his face. "Glad we got that squared away."

He heads for the door, but I halt him.

As happy as I am that we talked, our conversation still leaves me unsettled and there's something I really need him to know.

"Jace?"

"Yeah?"

"Stone isn't his brother."

The corner of his mouth curls and his stare turns glacial. "What makes you so sure?"

I tell him the truth.

"Because I wouldn't be with him if he was."

Chapter 32

"*L*ook at you," Stone declares as I walk up the stairs to his apartment. "No more crutches."

"It's a Christmas miracle." I do a little twirl when I reach him. "I still have to take it easy, but I'm glad I don't have to drag them around with me anymore."

Bending down, Stone kisses my lips. "I'm glad you're here."

"Me too." Palming his cheek, I pull him in for another kiss. "Merry Christmas."

"You're the best Christmas present ever," he murmurs against my lips.

I gesture to the present I'm holding. "In that case, I guess you don't want this, huh?"

I'm not sure what to make of the expression on his face. "You got me a gift?"

I bop him on the head with the box. "Of course, I did, silly." Placing it in his hands, I utter, "Open it."

"Right now?"

"Yes," I all but squeal.

I can't wait to see his face when he unwraps the autographed DVD of Bourne Identity.

"Holy shit." His eyes widen. "Is that Matt Damon's signature?"

I point to the other autograph next to it. "And the director's."

He wraps me up in a hug so tight it steals all the air from my lungs. "You're amazing, you know that?" His voice drops a fraction. "I feel shitty about not getting you anything now."

Well, this is awkward. Not because I'm upset that he didn't get me a gift—truth be told I never expected him to given his financial situation and all—but I know how Stone is and I don't want him to beat himself up about it.

"It's totally okay—" I start to say, but he cuts me off.

"I'm kidding, Bourne." He pulls a small box out of his pocket and hands it to me. "Of course I got you something."

"Can I open it here?"

"Yeah."

I break out in a grin as I tear open the gift wrapping…until I see what's inside.

A million different feelings hit me as I stare down at the Saint Christopher pendant on a silver chain.

"This is…" My breath stalls in my lungs. "I can't believe you did this."

He brushes my cheek with his thumb. "I know how much it meant to you and how upset you were when you realized it was gone."

I wasn't upset…I was utterly devastated.

It was as if my soul had been obliterated because I lost such a special piece of Liam.

My heartbeat kicks into high gear, a stampede of emotions pulling at my chest.

It's so thoughtful…so beautiful.

"I know it's not the same one Liam got you—"

"I love you," I whisper, my heart taking up residence in my throat.

The accident was an awful, horrible thing…but something good came out of it.

Him.

My eyes fill with tears as I peer up at him. "I really love you."

So much so I can't imagine ever not loving him.

His eyes crinkle at the corners as he fastens it around my neck. "I love you, too."

The kiss he gives me makes my toes curl and my heart soar.

"How did your attempt at dinner go?" I question as we pull apart.

He winces. "Well, that depends."

"On?"

"If you like your turkey well done or not."

Oh, boy.

A laugh bubbles out of my chest as we head for the door of his apartment. "Don't worry, I'm sure it's not too bad."

And if it is? Well, we can always order pizza.

I wait for him to open the door, but he doesn't.

"What's wrong?"

He looks down. "I should have told you before you left your house, but I got scared you wouldn't show, and I really wanted to give you your present."

The guilt on his face has my heart twisting. "What happened?"

His shoulders slump. "He told us he wasn't coming, but I guess he changed his mind."

"Who?"

"Tommy."

*I*t takes everything in me not to stab the son-of-a-bitch with my fork.

Tommy—who, quite frankly, looks like shit with his glazed-over eyes and disheveled appearance—laughs. "Can't believe you're dating a Covington."

Even his own mother looks annoyed with him. "Tommy, stop being rude to our guest."

It's not exactly an olive branch or anything, but I'll take it.

"Seriously?" he sneers. "Ma, our *guest* and her family spread a bunch of rumors about me and got me kicked out of school...after her brother attacked me in the woods." Tommy turns to me. "You know it wasn't my fault, right?" He shovels a forkful of food into his mouth. "Hell, I tried to help the kid by letting him see that his own brother was stabbing him in the back."

Head whirling, my hand tightens around my fork.

I'm going to kill him.

Stone helps himself to a second portion of stuffing. "You're one to talk."

Tommy rolls his eyes. "Don't tell me you're still upset about that Mercedes bitch. Like I said, I did you a favor." He winks at me. "Plus, you got yourself this fine piece of ass now."

The tendons in Stone's neck strain. "Shut up, Tommy."

Reaching over, Tommy slaps him on the back. "Relax, man. You know I'm just teasing." He zeros in on me again. "By the way, please send Dylan my condolences."

Needless to say, I'm confused. "Condolences for what?"

Winking, he shovels more food into his yap. "For shacking up with your piece of shit brother—"

"Jesus Christ," Stone snaps. "Will you shut the fuck up?"

I eye the knife Stone used to carve the burnt turkey and debate plunging it through his chest.

"You know what? You're right, I'm being a dick." He holds up his glass. "Let's toast to the happy couple."

Begrudgingly, Stone and his mom hold up their glasses.

I, however, don't move a muscle.

The douchebag notices. "Awe, come on." I want to wipe the stupid grin off his face. "Don't be like that. We're practically family now."

The piece of dog crap will never be my family.

Switching gears, he drawls, "For what it's worth, I'm happy you survived that car accident." He whistles. "Too bad that Hayley chick didn't. I heard they found her body parts scattered all over—"

My stomach recoils and I close my eyes.

"Thomas," his mother hisses. "We are at the dinner table."

"You're right, Ma. I'm sorry." Wiping his mouth with his napkin, he states, "Anyway, I heard you two used to dyke out—"

"Goddammit," Stone grunts, looking like he's a hair away from losing his shit entirely. "For fuck's sake, *stop*."

Finally, the asshole relents, turning his attention to his brother. "How's school going? Did you get into that pre-med program?"

Stone takes a lengthy sip of his drink. "I won't find out for another couple of months."

"Don't worry." He squeezes his shoulder. "You're smart as hell, brother. You got this."

Despite his irritation, Stone beams a little.

Tommy flicks his gaze to me. "But I'm guessing if he doesn't, you're gonna dump his ass, huh?"

Jesus. The nerve of him.

"You're…wow."

"What?" He points his fork at me. "We all know the only reason someone like you is with Stone is because he's going places."

He chews his food slowly, methodically. Like he's conjuring up his next brutal jab. Unfortunately, it's aimed at Stone.

"Don't come crying to me when she gets tired of slumming it and moves on to another sucker." Taking a sip of his beer, he narrows his eyes. "That's just how girls like *her* operate."

Stone looks down at his plate.

It's clear Tommy hit a nerve.

I thought I could do this. I figured if Stone could shoulder what my brothers put him through, I could be strong enough to withstand dealing with his.

But I can't.

Not when he's hurting someone I care about.

"You're a real piece of work, Tommy." Standing up, I toss my napkin in my dish. "I know you don't understand the concept because you have a cactus where your heart should be, but I'm in love with your brother. And neither you nor your stupid insults will change how I feel about him."

With that, I stalk off to the bathroom so I can splash some cool water on my face and remind myself that committing homicide is wrong.

J'm fixing my lipstick when the latch on the door clicks.

"I'll be done in a min—"

Words die in my throat when I see Tommy. "Well, if it isn't the little Covington whore."

I'm on my last thread with the douchebag. "Eat shit and die."

I go to brush past him, but he stands in front of the door, blocking it.

"Get out of my way."

He doesn't budge. "Relax. I just want to talk."

Somehow, I highly doubt that. "Fine. Let's talk about what an asshole—"

"Do you really love my brother?"

His question rattles me. Not because of what he's asking, but the sincerity behind it. As if he's actually concerned for Stone's welfare.

He doesn't deserve it, but I give him the truth anyway. "Yes." I meet his eyes. "I really do."

Blowing out a breath, he nods. "Okay."

I attempt to leave again but he presses me up against the sink, keeping me there with the force of his body.

"What the fuck are you doing?" I try to push him away, but he's stronger than I am. "Get the fuck off me."

He grips my ponytail so hard I yelp. "You and your brothers are scum, Covington. And if you think I'm gonna stand by and let you hurt my brother, you're out of your damn mind, bitch."

"Awe, don't worry, Tommy." I flash him some teeth. "Once I tell my brothers you attacked me, you won't be *standing* ever again."

His tongue finds his cheek. "Then I guess I better make this worth my while, huh?"

Bile rises up my throat as he shoves his hand up my skirt and slams his mouth against mine.

"What the fuck is going on here?"

Stone looks so hurt, so *betrayed*...it sucks all the oxygen out of the room.

"Like I said," Tommy sneers. "You can't trust a slut."

My stomach knots because I *know* how bad this looks.

I also know there's no way Stone will take my word against his own brother's.

Because I wouldn't.

I shake my head. "This isn't—"

I don't get a chance to finish my sentence, because Stone's fist flies into Tommy's face. "You, motherfucker."

Tommy tries to defend himself, but he's no match for the rage Stone unleashes on him. The next punch is so hard, blood trickles from his nose.

Gripping him by the collar of his shirt, Stone shoves his brother against a wall. "Don't ever fucking touch her again, you lying, piece of shit, junkie."

Woah.

I had no idea Tommy was on drugs, although it makes a whole lot of sense now. Not that it excuses any of his behavior.

Tommy starts coughing. "You're really gonna believe that little whore over your own brother?"

Stone's answer comes in the form of a sharp kick to the groin.

Tommy howls in pain, but Stone isn't finished with him yet.

He begins dragging him by his hair toward the front door. "We're fucking *done*. I'm tired of defending you. Tired of lending you money all the time. Tired of you destroying everything good in my life." His voice cracks. "Tired of being your brother."

Tommy tries to argue, but Stone pushes him out the door and deadbolts it.

"You can't kick me out." Tommy pounds on the door. "I'm your family."

Pain illuminates Stone's face and he closes his eyes, his body going slack against the frame. "Not anymore." He looks at his mom who's crying. "If you let him back in, I'm moving out."

She nods before disappearing in a fit of sobs.

Chest heaving, his gaze slides to me. "You okay?"

"Are *you?*"

I can't imagine how hard that must have been for him.

"Honestly?" He shakes his head. "Not really."

I wrap my arms around him, hugging him tight. "I didn't know he was on drugs."

"I didn't either," he whispers. "Not until recently."

"I'm so sorry."

It's all I've got because I don't know the right words to say or how to make any of this better for him.

"You have nothing to be sorry for." He cups my cheek. "Did he hurt you?"

"No." Not physically anyway. "I'm okay."

Thanks to *him.*

"Thank you for stopping him when you did."

For choosing me.

Wincing, he shakes out his hand. "Fucker has a hard-ass head."

He juts his chin toward the kitchen. "I'm gonna grab some ice."

While he does that, I take out my phone and start a group message with Jace and Cole.

I need them to know Stone is nothing like his brother.

Bianca: Stone just beat the shit out of Tommy.
Cole: That's surprising. Stone hits like a girl.
Jace: And you're telling us this because...

Irritation lodges in my throat as I type out my next text.

Bianca: Because he did it for me. Tommy cornered me in the bathroom and tried to attack me, but Stone protected me. He beat his ass and kicked him out of the house.

And his life.

A second later my phone vibrates and Jace's name illuminates my screen.

I swiftly pick it up.

"Hey—"

"Put Stone on the phone," Jace grinds out. "*Now.*"

The lethal tone of his voice makes it clear there's no room for argument.

On shaky legs, I walk over to Stone and hand him my cell. "Jace wants to talk to you."

Stone pinches the bridge of his nose. "Of course he does." He brings the phone to his ear. "Look, man. I already got into one fight today and I'm not looking for another—" His forehead creases. "Yeah, I did. What—" His jaw tics. "Because I love her."

There's a long pause...and then. "Okay."

I'm on the edge of my seat when he hangs up.

"What did he say?"

"He asked me if what you said was true...and then he asked me why I beat my brother up and kicked him out." Placing a bag of frozen peas on his wrist, he shrugs. "And then he said thank you and told me he wouldn't kick my ass the next time I drop you off."

Evidently, I got *two* miracles this Christmas.

Chapter 33

I snap my compact closed and stick it in my purse as my Uber comes to a stop in front of Cluck You.

"Thanks," I tell the driver as I step out of the car, my red heels clacking across the pavement.

Stone should be getting out of work any minute now—but since I'm still banned for life—I'm forced to wait outside for him.

The sound of someone whistling snags my attention.

I'm about to tell the asshole off, but when I turn around, I see Cole sitting in the driver's seat of Sawyer's van. Presumably waiting for her to get off work, too.

"You look fancy," he calls out.

Given I'm wearing one of old Bianca's expensive silk minidresses and it took me nearly two hours to get ready tonight I would hope so.

I walk over to the van. "It's my and Stone's three-month anniversary." I can't help but smile. "We're going out to dinner after his shift to celebrate."

I'd be lying if I said I wasn't excited about actually going out somewhere for once.

I'm also excited to tell him I was accepted into the psychology program at Duke's Heart. My former self and I might differ, but psychology seems to be something we both love.

Whatever smart-ass retort Cole wanted to make falls by the wayside, and I'm appreciative.

Stone and my brothers aren't exactly friends and I doubt they'll ever be close, but at least he's allowed inside the house now and they've stopped threatening to kill him whenever they cross paths.

"Well, we might as well wait for them together." Cole gestures to the passenger seat. "Come on in."

A smell that can only be described as heavenly hits my nostrils as I climb into the passenger seat. "God, that smells so good."

"Dude, I *know*," Cole agrees with a pout. "It seriously fucking sucks that I'm forbidden to have any." His pout deepens. "Mr. Gonzales won't even let Sawyer give me a doggie bag."

I know the feeling. Stone isn't allowed to bring home any leftovers either which sucks because I'm dying to know if it tastes even half as good as it smells.

"Tell me about it." I give him a pointed look. "And I mean that in the literal sense because I can't remember ever eating here."

Humming, he rests his head against the seat. "Oh, man. Best fried chicken I've *ever* had. Moist and crispy...perfect crunch when you bite into it."

My stomach grumbles. *Damn.*

"Fucking amazeballs." Giving his head a small shake, he laughs. "Jace, Oakley, and I used to come here after we'd smoke—"

"Oakley?" I question because I don't recall hearing the name before. "Is that a friend of yours?"

The smile wipes clean off his face. "Yeah." A mixture of sadness and sorrow flicker in his green eyes. "Yeah...he was."

I'm about to ask what happened, but Cole shoots his gaze out the windshield and beams. "There's my girl."

A bubbly, albeit visibly exhausted Sawyer walks over to Cole's side of the van and gives him a kiss. "Your very tired girl." She yawns. "Working back-to-back doubles kicked my butt." She looks at me. "Stone will be out any minute. One of the dishwashers broke and he's fixing it."

I inwardly shiver as I imagine him crouched over, sleeves pushed up his forearms, with a tool in his hand.

There's something so hot about a man who knows how to repair stuff.

"How was your day?" Sawyer asks my brother.

Cole starts to tell her, but Sawyer yawns again.

Eyes wide with remorse, she slams a hand over her mouth. "Lord, that was rude of me. I'm sorry."

Cole doesn't look offended at all. "How about we get you home and into bed?" I don't miss the way his eyes gleam when he says the last word.

Gross.

Sawyer nods emphatically. "Yes, please."

After trading places with Sawyer and exchanging goodbyes with them, I spot Stone walking out of Cluck You.

Running over, I wrap my arms around him. "Happy Anniversary."

Body going slack, he squeezes me tight and breathes me in...as if he needed this hug more than his next heartbeat.

"Everything okay?"

I'm not sure what to make of his expression when we break apart, but he's definitely not happy.

"No." Frowning, he looks down at his shoes. "I didn't get into the pre-med program." He snorts. "They fucking waitlisted me."

Oh, shit.

The crestfallen look on his face punches straight through my heart.

However, hope isn't lost just yet.

"I know it sucks getting waitlisted, but there's still a chance—"

"No, there isn't," he snaps. "You think Duke's Heart is going to take some dirt-poor motherfucker like me over a bunch of rich assholes whose parents have connections?" Head hanging low, he ambles to his car. "I fucking knew this was gonna happen. Don't even know why I bothered trying to begin with."

He tried because he wants better for himself.

He tried because he's determined and hard-working.

He tried because he's not the type to give up, despite whatever obstacles are in his way.

It's just one of the many reasons I love him.

Framing his face with my hands, I utter, "You're amazing and smart—"

"Stop." He removes my hands. "I don't need or want your pity."

It's not pity…it's *love*.

But he's so upset right now, feeling like the universe is against him, he can't tell them apart.

"Stone?"

"What?" he grinds out.

"What can I do?"

Because there has to be *something*.

Dark brows snap together and his shoulders hunch. "Nothing." Turning to his car, he gets inside. "I just want to be left alone."

I ignore the disappointment in my chest as the engine roars to life.

"Get in. I'll drop you off at home."

Part of me wants to argue because I don't want to leave him alone tonight, but I think there might be a way I can help him after all.

I know Stone loathes rich kids whose parents have connections… but his girlfriend happens to be one of them.

And she's going to use it to *his* advantage.

"*I*s Dad home?" I ask Jace as I pass him on the staircase. "Yeah, actually. He's in his office." I continue up the stairs, but he stops me. "I saw your acceptance letter from Duke's Heart on the kitchen table." His face lights up. "I'm proud—"

"Can we catch up later, Jace? I really need to talk to Dad."

As happy as I am to be attending college with my brothers and their girls, I can't celebrate quite yet.

Not until I know Stone will be there too.

He blinks. "Yeah…sure. Is everything okay?"

"No, but it will be."

Brushing past him, I sprint up the stairs and into my father's office.

"Hey, Dad. Do you have a minute?"

He presses a button on his phone. "For you? I have a million." Speaking back into the receiver, he says, "Nadia, darling. I'll have to call you back in a bit. Bianca needs to talk to me." He smiles. "I love you."

Hearing him tell another woman who isn't my mother that he loves her should probably make me angry, but it's hard when I see how happy Nadia makes him.

My chest knots.

He deserves someone who loves him unconditionally.

After hanging up with Nadia, he looks at me. "What's up, sweetheart?"

Heart beating fast, I walk over to the empty chair across from his desk and take a seat. I haven't worked out what to say exactly, but my father is the best person to help me because he owns the largest pharmaceutical company in the country...which means he has *a lot* of connections in the medical industry.

"My boyfriend, Stone——"

His green eyes narrow. "The DaSilva boy."

It takes everything in me not to scream because the one thing Jace, Cole, and my father all seem to agree on is that I should *never* be allowed to have a boyfriend.

"Yes, Stone DaSilva." I can't help but fidget because I'm nervous. "He applied to the pre-med program at Duke's Heart."

My father seems impressed. "Good for him. It's a tough program, but also one of the very best in the nation. Lots of great doctors come out of there."

I sit up straight. "I know, and he worked so hard for it." I lick my dry lips. "However, he found out today that he was waitlisted."

He rubs his chin, assessing me. "Okay."

Time to stop talking in circles and get to the point. "I guess I was hoping...you know, with all of your connections——"

"You want me to see if I can get him into the program," he concludes with a sigh.

I draw in a breath. "Yes."

It feels like an eternity before he speaks. "Bianca, you know I love you, but asking me to do a favor for some boy——"

"He isn't some boy, Dad." I stand, my frustration rising. "I love him." Crossing my arms over my chest, I stare him down. "Stone is the hardest working person I've ever met, and he *deserves* to be in that program." I punch my finger into the mahogany wood of his desk. "All I'm asking for is a phone call so they give him a chance." I throw my hands up. "But if you don't want to help me, it's fine. Because I *will* figure out another way to make it happen."

Stone's dreams are my dreams and come hell or high water, he's getting into that program.

"Wow," my dad whispers.

I glare at him. "Wow, *what?*"

He sits there—staring at me—for what feels like an eternity before he finally speaks. "You remind me so much of your mother right now. She was always so passionate about the things—the people—she believed in."

My muscles lock up and my heart seizes. "Oh."

Scrubbing a hand down his face, he leans back in his chair. "This young man is really important to you, huh?"

I look him right in the eyes. "I wouldn't be here asking for your help if he wasn't."

A long-defeated sigh escapes him. "I'll make a few phone calls tomorrow."

Chapter 34

$\mathcal{I}$ can barely contain the excitement coursing through me when Stone opens the door to his apartment.

He doesn't know it yet, but my dad was able to get him into the pre-med program.

They'll be sending out his acceptance letter this afternoon, but I wanted to be the first person to tell him.

He perks up a bit when he sees me. "Hey——"

"I have to tell you something, but I need you to promise me you won't get upset," I blurt out.

I know how Stone is and I don't want him to get upset that my family pulled some strings. I want him to be happy, because strings or no strings, he's earned this.

He raises an eyebrow. "Okay." He gestures for me to follow him into his bedroom. "Not gonna lie, though. You're kind of scaring me."

"Don't be scared," I tell him, closing the door behind us. "It's a good thing." I grin so hard it hurts. "A *really* good thing."

"Well, if that's the case can you spit it out already, Bourne? The suspense is killing me."

Right.

"Well, the other night I talked to my dad and told him that you were waitlisted and how it wasn't fair...and he agreed."

It's not quite the truth, but close enough.

The air in my lungs grows thin as I gather the courage to tell him the most important part. "He ended up making a few phone calls and… you're officially enrolled in the pre-med program at Duke's Heart."

I brace myself for him to start yelling, but he doesn't.

In fact, it's a good thing he's sitting on his bed now because he looks like he's about to pass out.

"Holy shit," he says after a minute. "Are you *serious?*"

I nod. I nod so hard I'm surprised my head doesn't fall off. "Yes. They're mailing out your acceptance letter today and everything. I just wanted to be the first person to tell you because I know how much this means to you."

Rushing toward me, he hoists me off the ground so fast I squeal.

"Thank you." He peppers kisses along my cheeks, my lips, my forehead. "Holy fucking shit. I can't believe I'm in."

Whatever anxiety I was harboring about Stone being mad dissipates as I wrap my legs around his waist. "I love you."

Walking us toward the bed, he sits us down. "I love *you.*"

There's so much joy on his face, my heart takes flight. "You deserve this, Stone."

He kisses me slow and deep, like I'm the most precious thing in the world. "You're amazing, Bianca."

"So are you."

Desire shadows his eyes before he kisses me again, his tongue spearing mine.

My chest heaves, my nipples grazing his chest with each breath I draw in as he continues kissing me into oblivion.

Groaning, he shifts so he's lying on top of me. I instinctively part my thighs and he situates himself between them.

Goosebumps break out along my flesh as he grinds against the spot that lights all my nerve endings on fire.

My fingers grip the hem of my shirt and I slip it over my head, needing fewer clothes and more skin between us.

Stone squeezes my breast with one hand, while his other goes to the zipper of my jeans. "Is this okay?"

I slide them down my hips before kicking them off. "More than okay."

"Good."

My panties follow suit a moment later.

"Jesus, Bourne." His gaze darkens with lust as he stares down at my exposed sex. "You're so damn beautiful."

I tug on the elastic of his sweatpants and his dick springs out, hard and ready for me.

"Stone?"

His throat bobs on a swallow. "Yeah?"

I peer up at him. "I want you inside me."

Stone's been patient, never pushing me for anything I wasn't ready for, but this feels right.

So fucking right.

I wrap my fingers around him, giving his dick a slow jerk as he fishes out a condom from his nightstand. "Are you sure?"

"Positive."

My mouth goes dry, want and need coiling through me as I watch him roll it over his length.

And that's when it occurs to me.

"I can't remember ever having sex," I utter aloud as he lines himself up with my entrance.

Stone stills, my confession visibly confusing him. "Are you a virgin?"

I shouldn't laugh, it's not funny. But the thought of former me being a virgin is downright laughable given what I know about her.

Hell, I probably screwed half the town.

"I don't think so," I whisper.

But my past—who I used to be—it no longer matters. *Not anymore.*

"Should I stop?" Stone questions.

The head of his cock nudges me, desperate to get inside.

"No." Spreading my legs wider, I run my hand along his jaw. "I want to make new memories."

With him.

"I love you," he rasps, slowly sliding inside me.

The first thrust is so different, so unfamiliar and new, it steals my breath.

"Are you okay?" Stone whispers, tiny beads of sweat breaking out along his brow.

"Better than okay." I press my hands to his back, urging him on. "Keep going."

And he does, fucking me in slow, steady strokes that have us both sucking in air like it's our last.

"You feel so good," he rasps. "So fucking good."

Stone's mouth finds mine mid-thrust. His kiss is demanding and needy, as if he can't get enough. "Tell me you love me."

"I love you," I breathe, running my nails up and down his back.

He thrusts again, harder this time. His eyes turning near black with need. "Tell me you want me."

Our gazes collide. "I want you."

The declaration has him grunting as his movements pick up speed. I can feel his body straining and his muscles coiling, his breaths now coming out in short, frantic pants. "Oh, fuck."

My thighs clench. I'm so close to coming, I can practically taste my impending orgasm.

Reaching between us, I impatiently circle my clit.

A breathy moan escapes me, my legs shaking as the tension releases and ripples of pleasure shoot through my body.

A second later, Stone groans my name before he collapses on top of me. "That was amazing."

I make a hum of agreement in my throat as I catch my breath and he gets off the bed.

I take in his naked form as I watch him deposit the condom in the trash can.

"You have a cute butt," I comment when he joins me in bed again.

A laugh escapes him, and the sound is like music to my ears. "Thanks." He folds his arms around me, tucking me to his chest. "I still can't believe I got in."

I decide now is the perfect time to share my own good news. "I didn't tell you before, but I got accepted into the psychology program at Duke's Heart."

Grinning, he peers down at me. "This is seriously the best day ever."

"I know." I skim my fingertips along his stomach. "I heard they have co-ed dorms on campus, so maybe we can—"

"I can't dorm on campus." His face falls. "My financial aid only covers the classes."

My heart sinks. There goes *that* idea.

Unless…

"Let me talk to my dad again, his company gives out grants and—"

"No," Stone barks, sitting up in bed. "I don't need your daddy to come to the rescue again."

Wow. That hurts. *A lot.*

I hug the sheets tighter around me. "Calm down, Stone. I was just trying to figure out a way we could live close to one another since our schedules will be hectic next year and we'll barely have time to see each other."

A horrifying thought hits me. *Maybe distance is what he wants.*

I mentally slap my face because that's crazy talk. Stone's given me no indication that he wants to end things.

Quite the contrary actually.

"I know." Jumping to his feet, Stone shuffles back into his sweatpants. "Which is exactly why I want you to move in here."

I stare at him, silently pondering if the sex we just had scrambled his brain.

"You want me to move in *here*?" I repeat, making sure I understood him.

"Yeah." Scoffing, he places a hand over his heart. "Oh, I'm sorry, princess. Is this apartment not good enough for you?"

The apartment is fine…it's the woman who gave birth to him living in it that might pose a potential problem.

"Your mom doesn't even like me," I hiss. "Therefore, I'm pretty sure she'd hate the idea of me living here."

He looks offended. "My mom likes you just fine."

That's a heaping pile of bullshit.

"You know, I might actually believe that if the woman ever bothered to say more than two words to me."

Hell, his *neighbors* talk to me more than she does.

"She's always been quiet." Narrowing his eyes, he points a finger at me. "Stop thinking you're so goddamn special that people need to roll out the red carpet and kiss your ass whenever you appear."

Pure rage sears through my belly and I climb out of his bed and search for my clothes because arguing when you're stark naked feels weird.

"Stop treating me like I'm some kind of snobby brat when you know I'm not like that." I shimmy into my jeans. "Bottom line, even if your mom did like me—which she *doesn't*. I want to live on campus so I can have the full college experience." I open my arms wide. "But, hey—fuck me for wanting my boyfriend to be a part of that, right?"

His jaw tics. "Bianca—"

"Just let my dad give you the grant, Stone." I pull my shirt over my head. "This way we can—"

"I'm not your goddamn charity case!" he roars so loud I jump. "Unlike you and the rest of your rich, pampered, stuck-up family, I don't need your daddy to hand me everything on a silver platter."

It would hurt less if he slapped me across the face.

My brothers and I might be well off thanks to our dad, but we work hard for the things we want.

Hell, I busted my ass to maintain my good grades so I could get into the psych program. Jace works his brain and fingers to the bone creating video games and has never accepted a dime from my dad past the age of fourteen. And Cole works his ass off on the football field—suffering through grueling games and practices all while pushing his body to limits most aren't capable of—day in and day out.

The fact that Stone just reduced us to a bunch of pretentious, superficial, high and mighty assholes, shows what he really thinks about us.

It also makes him a hypocrite.

"You needed my *daddy* to get into the pre-med program," I bite out before I can stop myself.

I immediately regret the words the second they leave my mouth, but it's too late.

"Wow." He flinches, his jaw bunching tight. "Didn't take long for you to hold that over my head, huh?"

Dammit. That was a low blow. One I truly didn't mean, but he shouldn't have said those things either.

"I'm sor—"

"Fuck you," he seethes.

Whatever. I'm not going to stand here and keep apologizing to him if he's going to be like *that*.

I grab my purse off the floor. "I'm going home."

He regards me like I'm nothing more than garbage on the side of the road. "Good."

It's tragic how in the blink of an eye, the best day can turn into the worst.

Chapter 35

The knock on my bedroom door lulls me from the constant loop of thoughts running through my mind.

The mean things Stone said.

The cruel things I said back.

How loving someone so much gives them the power to hurt you.

And how ironic it is that the only person who can fix my broken pieces is the same one responsible for causing the damage in the first place.

"Come in," I croak out, my voice hoarse from all the crying I've been doing.

Everything was perfect with Stone and I…

Until it wasn't.

The door opens, revealing a concerned Jace on the other side. "Your boyfriend's downstairs." Hands tucked into the pockets of his jeans, he ambles inside my room. "He looks like someone killed his dog. What happened?"

That's the thing…I don't even know.

One second we were making love—*soaring*—while sharing this amazing moment together…and the next we were crashing.

It's as if my heart is on a constant roller-coaster ride.

The lows are brutal, but the highs are so great—so addicting—it's worth the price of admission.

But is it?—a tiny voice in the back of my head whispers.

Ignoring that negative voice—because nothing good ever comes from it—I peer up at my brother. "We got into a fight."

Jace gives me a pointed look, as if he can see right through the bullshit in that way only the people who truly care about you can. "I figured as much." He takes a seat on the edge of my bed. "What did you guys fight about?"

I'm not sure how to answer that. I can't tell him about asking our father to get Stone into the pre-med program because Jace already paints Stone in a bad light and I don't want to add fuel to the fire.

I, can, however, give him part of the truth.

The part that matters.

"Stone got accepted into the pre-med program at Duke's Heart," I begin. "And since I got into Duke's Heart, too, I brought up the possibility of us moving into a co-ed dorm, so we'd be able to see each other more. However, Stone said his financial aid doesn't cover dorms." I draw in a deep breath. "So, I simply mentioned that Dad's company gives out grants and I could get him one…but then he freaked out and accused me of making him a charity case."

Jace rubs his chin, appearing lost in thought before he speaks. "Well, as much as I want to take your side…I can also see where he's coming from."

To say I'm surprised—and a little offended—would be an understatement. "You're kidding, right? What's the big deal about him taking the grant money?"

Especially if it enables us to see each other more. Because isn't *that* what matters most at the end of the day?

Jace laughs. "Because men have a little something called pride." His expression turns serious. "We want to take care of our girl and support her…not the other way around."

He's got to be kidding me. "Wow, that's a little sexist."

"It's not sexist," he argues. "Men are biologically wired to take care of ourselves *and* take care of what's ours. It's just the way we love." His brows draw tight. "And while Stone might not be my favorite person in the world, I do respect his strong work ethic." He winces. "That said—it's gotta be a pretty big blow to the ego if you're struggling financially, and your girl suggests that her rich daddy swoop in to fix everything because you're not able to give her what she wants…even though she meant well."

I never really thought about it like that, although I probably should have. Stone's all about taking care of the people he loves.

It's just one of the reasons I love him.

I get off my bed. "I'm gonna go downstairs and talk to him."

Jace starts to say something, but I don't hear him because I make a mad dash for the staircase.

I find Stone standing by the front door, looking so sad and hurt, my heart recoils.

"I'm sorry," we both say at the same time.

A lump rises in my throat. "I didn't mean—"

"No. I was the one who was wrong," Stone interjects. "I lashed out when you were only trying to help me." He takes a step in my direction. "But the moment you left I realized something important…something I won't ever forget."

My heart kicks up a notch as he takes another step. "What?"

"The love I have for you is more important than anything… including my pride." A determined note enters his voice. "Because I *can't* lose you, Bianca. I refuse to."

"I don't want to lose you either."

"Good." The groove in his forehead deepens. "I'm not taking that grant money, but if you really want to dorm on campus, I won't stop you." He tilts my chin. "Because I want you to have everything you want."

I meet his eyes, my heart skipping a beat. "What I want is you."

He closes the distance between us, kissing me with so much adoration my knees go weak.

"Promise me you're mine," he whispers against my lips. "Promise me you'll *always* be mine and that we'll get through anything life throws at us."

As usual, Stone has this way of making me feel like I'm going to miss out on the opportunity of a lifetime if I don't go along for the ride.

But I want this.

I peer up at him. "I promise."

Because when you love someone—really love them—you can't see a future without them.

Even if you can't remember your past.

Epilogue

Three Months Later...

"*R*eady to graduate?" Jace asks from the entryway of my bedroom.

I give myself one final look in the mirror. "One second."

Picking up a tube of red lipstick on my vanity, I apply some.

Not for me, but for old Bianca. She worked hard for this moment, and this is my small way of sharing it with her.

"Man, it's so weird seeing you in that thing," Cole comments, standing next to Jace.

I turn to look at him. "My cap and gown?"

"No." He sweeps a hand up and down. "A *red* cap and gown instead of the blue ones we wore."

"We're still proud of you, though," Jace says while staring at his watch. "But hurry the fuck up because Dad, Sawyer, and Dylan are waiting in the car and we're already five minutes late."

I quickly blot my lips with a tissue. "Ready."

"Hold on," Cole says. "I gotta get the gun out of the safe."

My mouth drops open. "What? Why?"

He blinks as if the answer should be obvious. "For protection."

"Oh, for fuck's sake," Jace mutters while pinching the bridge of his nose. "You're not bringing a gun to Bianca's graduation."

Cole sulks. "Fine. But don't bitch to me when someone threatens to bust a cap in your ass."

I can't help but laugh because my family is crazy.

But I love them.

$\mathcal{M}$y phone vibrates with an incoming text the moment my butt hits the seat.

Stone: You looked beautiful up there.

A smile stretches across my lips as I text him back.

Bianca: So did you.
Stone: You know you're the best thing that ever happened to me, right?

My pulse kicks up a few notches. Stone can be so sweet sometimes he takes my breath away.

Bianca: I'm pretty sure it's the other way around.

I watch dots form at the bottom of my screen before they disappear completely.

Bianca: Come on, DaSilva. Don't hold out on me. What's on your mind?
Stone: You.

My cheeks heat as I look down the row.

Tilting his head ever-so-slightly, he looks my way.

I'm not sure what to make of his expression, but he seems nervous, which of course puts me on edge.

I quickly type out my next text.

Bianca: Good things, I hope.

Stone: Always.

Relief flows through me and I'm about to respond, but my phone vibrates with another text.

Stone: I can't believe we graduated.

A bittersweet twist goes through my chest.

Bianca: I know. Even though I can't remember the last four years, it's crazy to know it's all over.

The announcer at the podium motions for us to stand so we can move our tassels.

I quickly push to my feet, my thumbs still hovering over the keyboard of my phone.

Bianca: It feels like the end of something huge.

Joining my classmates, I switch my tassel to the other side of my cap.

A moment later we throw them in the air and everyone cheers.

"Or is it the beginning?" Stone says behind me.

I quickly turn around. "What—"

My heart's in my throat as Stone pulls out what looks like a jewelry box...right before he gets down on one knee.

"Bianca Covington, will you marry me?"

Untitled

DYLAN

Warning: Proceed with caution.

I rub my sweaty palms on my jeans as I take a seat on the other side of the glass and wait for them to bring him out.

The sound of the heavy door creaking open makes my nerves jump like hot oil in a pan.

I really don't want to be the one to tell him this...but he has a right to know.

My stomach bottoms out when I see him shuffle through the door in his orange jumpsuit.

His hair is a little longer, and the stubble on his face is at least a week old...but it's his eyes that send a pang of sorrow through my heart.

They're dimmer...like being in this place sucked the life right out of them.

Out of him.

And what I'm about to say will only make his misery worse.

But I can't not tell him.

He picks up the phone on his end and brings it to his ear as he sits down. "I told you not to come." His voice is a broken rasp, much like he is. "I don't want you seeing me here."

You'd think he'd know me better than that.

"And I told *you* we were family, Oakley."

Preorder Broken Kingdom today!

Want to be notified about my upcoming releases?https://goo.gl/n5Azwv

Royal Hearts Academy

Series Order:
Cruel Prince (Jace's Book)
Ruthless Knight (Cole's Book)
Wicked Princess (Bianca's Book)
Broken Kingdom

Join my newsletter and sign up for the latest news, updates on my books, and new releases:

http://signup.ashleyjadeauthor.com/

About the Author

Want to be notified about my upcoming releases? https://goo.gl/n5Azwv

Ashley Jade craves tackling different genres and tropes within romance. Her first loves are New Adult Romance and Romantic Suspense, but she also writes everything in between including: contemporary romance, erotica, and dark romance.

Her characters are flawed and complex, and chances are you will hate them before you fall head over heels in love with them.

She's a die-hard lover of oxford commas, em dashes, music, coffee, and anything thought provoking...except for math.

Books make her heart beat faster and writing makes her soul come alive. She's always read books growing up and scribbled stories in her journal, and after having a strange dream one night; she decided to just go for it and publish her first series.

It was the best decision she ever made.

If she's not paying off student loan debt, working, or writing a novel—you can usually find her listening to music, hanging out with her readers online, and pondering the meaning of life.

Check out her social media pages for future novels.

She recently became hip and joined Twitter, so you can find her there, too.

She loves connecting with her readers—they make her world go round'.

~Happy Reading~

Feel free to email her with any questions / comments: ashleyjadeauthor@gmail.com

For more news about what I'm working on next: Follow me on my Facebook page: https://www.facebook.com/pages/Ashley-Jade/788137781302982

Other Books Written By Ashley Jade

The Devil's Playground Duet (Books 1 & 2)

Complicated Parts - Series (Books 1 & 2 Out Now)

Complicated Hearts - Duet (Books 1 & 2)

Blame It on the Shame - Trilogy (Parts 1-3)

Blame It on the Pain - Standalone

Thanks for Reading!
Please follow me online for more.
<3 Ashley Jade

Made in the USA
Columbia, SC
16 April 2024

c7c3f8b9-6e29-40e1-bbd5-5bd676315612R02